To

Indianapolis and

Marion County.

All best wishes,
John R. Riggs

MUCH MADNESS

JOHN R. RIGGS

authorHOUSE®

AuthorHouse™
1663 Liberty Drive
Bloomington, IN 47403
www.authorhouse.com
Phone: 1 (800) 839-8640

Published by AuthorHouse 01/22/2018

ISBN: 978-1-5462-2502-7 (sc)
ISBN: 978-1-5462-2503-4 (e)

Library of Congress Control Number: 2018900935

Print information available on the last page.

Much Madness is divinest Sense
To a discerning Eye –
Much Sense – the starkest Madness

Emily Dickinson

To Carole;
And those of you who have been with me
Every step of the way

Chapter 1

It was one of those blue-and-white, mid-March days that look a whole lot better from inside the house than they feel once outside in the wind. I had been seduced by the bright patch of sunlight shining on our dining room floor into wearing only a crew sweatshirt over my T-shirt on my trip to the farm, and now, while standing in the shade, sans watch cap and windbreaker, regretted my optimism. But optimism is like that. It wears well until it wears thin, and provides us with most of our shining, and bitter, moments. The moment at hand was neither shining nor bitter. Just perplexing.

I am Garth Ryland, owner, publisher, and editor of the *Oakalla Reporter,* a weekly newspaper located in the small town of Oakalla, Wisconsin, which is about a forty-five mile drive from downtown Madison via what we natives call Madison Road. The *Reporter* and I are both dinosaurs in that we are creatures of the past, born in an age when print was king, and people had the time, and took the time, to sit down with their family, eat a meal, and read a newspaper—sometimes twice a day. Neither do we fit the current climate of tweet and anti-tweet, sound bites and political correctness. Yet here we both are, still alive and kicking, simply because we refuse to die. Not that I couldn't do anything else. I just don't want to. Not that the *Reporter* is a money tree. It is far from it. But I love what I do, which is working by, and for, myself to try to give honest voice to the people of Oakalla, to report their lives and tell their stories, and as much as it is within my power, be a force for good. If that sounds like so much hokum, so be it. But also be assured: I am not Andy Griffith. Oakalla is not Mayberry.

The reason that I was at the farm was to take inventory to see what needed doing in case Abby and I wanted to move here, following our wedding in July. Abby is Abby Airhart, the love of my life and currently employed by the University of Wisconsin, Madison to teach a class in pathology. She is also a surgeon in the emergency room at University Hospital, and a very nice person. Ours has been a long courtship that has stretched across the miles and years, bent, but never broken, and when she came back to Oakalla in January, it was to stay. It seems moot to say, I was delighted.

The problem we now faced was where to live once we were married. I didn't want to live at her house that doubled as a shelter for abused women and where she was now living. She didn't want to come live with Ruth and me at my house. With good reason, I might add, because I didn't want to live with Abby, Ruth and me at my house. That either left the farm or buying another house in town, which seemed a huge waste of money, even if we could afford it. The problem with the farm, as I had discovered as I took inventory, was that it hadn't been occupied for many years, and while I kept it in good repair in the meantime, it would still take a lot of work to make it our home. More than I wanted to undertake, because essentially nothing had changed since

Grandmother Ryland died, except for the bats in the attic, the gaps around the windows, the cracked plaster on the ceilings, the piled dust on the furnishings, and the mouse crap everywhere. The second problem with the farm was that I was not a country boy at heart. I knew that I could once again learn to love it there, as I had during the idles of my youth, when I spent my summers there. And there were those legions of city dwellers who, once they moved to the country, vowed never to move back to town again. But I liked living in town. I liked walking to work and walking to lunch and visiting with the townspeople and all the gossip and comradery that came with it. Once I moved to the country, I feared I would become more aloof and less caring about the citizens of Oakalla, and more inclined to sit at my window and watch life go by than take the pulse of my neighbors. I really wasn't a people person, and yet I was. The years had made me so. And while I likely could retire to the country with ease, I couldn't yet quit town. Not as long as I had a newspaper to run.

That, however, wasn't what currently occupied my attention. The large brass Yale padlock that secured the hasp of the root cellar door was my focus. The padlock was not original equipment. Neither had I put it there.

It was a short walk to the machinery shed where Grandmother Ryland had once parked her car and green International pickup, and kept her tools in a long narrow room at the north end of it. The room had a set of narrow steps that led to a loft that looked out (when its wooden shutters were open) a wide window at the rest of the farm. The loft had always intrigued me—not because of what was there, which was mainly an assortment of old household

3

items, zinc wash tubs, copper boilers, and the like, but because I could never gauge its purpose. It seemed too well planned for random storage and yet too lightly used for anything else. One of life's enduring mysteries, I guessed, because I never thought to ask either my grandmother Ryland or my father when they were alive what its exact purpose was, and now that they were dead, there was no one left who could tell me.

The machinery shed smelled like prairie dirt as old as earth itself. I still caught a whiff of it sometimes while driving Jessie, the now ancient Chevy sedan that I had inherited from Grandmother along with the farm and the money to buy the *Reporter*. As a boy, I would never stay in the shed for more than a few minutes at a time for fear of wrecking my lungs. That was in contrast to the barn where I spent many a happy hour building hay forts and shooting sparrows with my B-B gun. The shed was probably better for my lungs than the barn, but as a kid, I didn't know that. Or care to know that. I was too busy enjoying life to think beyond my instincts, and hay smelled better to me than dirt. Still did for that matter. I grabbed a large pair of bolt cutters and a wrecking bar in case the bolt cutters wouldn't cut brass and got out of there.

It turned out the bolt cutters would cut brass, if I put my full weight on them. And strained a few muscles in the bargain. One of those things born out of need, like climbing a ladder to clean your gutters, that you know you probably ought not do, but do anyway, and then vow never to do again—until the next time it needs done.

The root cellar also had an earthy smell to it, but not one I found unpleasant. Maybe the hundreds of cans of fruits and vegetables that it had housed over the years had mellowed it, or maybe because I still associated it with the huckster wagon and the bottled pop that it once brought on a hot summer day that led me on a trip down the cellar steps to sit in the cool and drink my cream soda. Ever after, I had always felt comfortable in there, even when Annie Lawson locked the door behind me on that bitterly cold late December night that nearly cost both of us our lives.

Strange to be warm again now that I was out of the wind. Strange to see all those Mason jars filled with canned goods still lining the shelves. Stranger yet to see the large wooden box on the floor in front of me. The lid was nailed shut, so I put the wrecking bar to good use.

I knew what I would find even before the lid was all the way off. A corpse has an unmistakable odor to it that once experienced, always leaves one breathless. I leaned away from the box, took a gulp of air, and finished removing the lid. Another gulp of air later, I looked inside the box and saw what appeared in the dim light to be a human skeleton. Further examination showed no trace of clothing or meat on the bones. Even the air from the box was growing sweeter by the second now that the lid was off until I hardly noticed it.

Normally I would have found the nearest phone, called Ben Bryan, the county coroner, and dumped box, skeleton, and all in his lap. But Ben and his wife, Faye, were spending the winter in Panama City Beach, Florida, and wouldn't be home until the first of April at the earliest, depending on, in his words, "how the weather is up there." That left Adams County without a coroner, as we were left without a sheriff years ago, or an Oakalla town marshal after Cecil Hardwick resigned. State policeman Michael Higgins had filled the gap admirably in a lot of ways, but after his death in December, we had been left adrift again, and would be until the County Council got its act together and either appointed someone sheriff, or held a special election to elect one. But the County Council was in no hurry to do either, which left me with my Special Deputy badge to handle what the state police would not, and Abby to fill in for Ben Bryan until his return. She was much more qualified to do her job than I mine, in fact overqualified, but that still didn't change my situation any. I wasn't a lawman in any way, shape, or form, and had no desire to be one. I longed for that day when Rupert Roberts was sheriff, and in charge, and I the new kid on the block, which was the same as longing for those simpler, happier times of childhood—an utter and complete waste of time.

I got in Jessie and started the two mile drive back to Oakalla. I had planned to stop by Fair Haven Cemetery on the way home to pay my respects to an old friend of mine, but didn't think it prudent under the circumstances, especially since someone seemed to be following me, and had been since I left the farm. I didn't know for certain that was the case, but every time I looked in Jessie's rear view mirror, I saw someone there, and just far enough back that I couldn't make out any details concerning the vehicle he was driving. It looked like a black pickup to me, but it could have been a navy blue SUV, or an olive green Hummer, or a Zero on its way to an air show. I couldn't tell, and there was no way, short of stopping in the middle of the road, to find out. Finally, I did just that, only to see the vehicle turn around in a farm field and go the other way. Point proved, I guessed. Whatever the point was.

Danny Palmer was to my mind the next best thing since indoor plumbing. He owned and operated the Marathon Service Station, was an ace mechanic, volunteer fire chief, school board president, a member of the town council, and a deacon in his church. But his greatest accomplishment, much to my chagrin, was that he had kept Jessie running lo these many years. Not well, mind you. No one could do that. But running. Which was the only thing that had kept me from giving her the deep six long ago.

Danny was at work changing someone's oil. Sniffy Smith, my barber and a daily resident of the Marathon now that he was retired, was keeping Danny company atop his favorite stool where he liked to shell and eat peanuts while waxing poetic. I hated the thought of Oakalla without either one of them—Danny for his friendship and his service, and Sniffy for his large, often misguided, heart and comic relief. The point was often lost that Sniffy sometimes had a point because he was equally as adamant in his argument when wrong, as when right, and would never admit otherwise. But I liked him just the same. Some people you do, regardless.

"Afternoon, Garth." Sniffy had emptied his bowl of peanuts and was scanning the floor in case he'd dropped one. "What's going on? You look like you just saw a ghost."

Sometimes Sniffy was far more perceptive than I wanted him to be. "I just came from the farm and need Danny's help in retrieving something."

7

"An old treasure?" Try though he might, Sniffy was not good at feigning indifference. If he'd leaned any farther forward, he would have fallen off the chair. Even his ears seemed pointed in my direction.

"You might say that, although it's hard to estimate its worth."

A secret was not something Sniffy could keep if his life depended on it. Danny, on the other hand, knew as many of Oakalla's secrets as I, and it was that shared burden that bonded and defined us. We knew too much about Oakalla and each other to be anything but friends.

"When do you want to go?" Danny rolled his four-wheel cart out from under the car, stood, and wiped his hands on a grease rag.

"Whenever you're ready."

"How long is it going to take?"

"About as long as it takes to drive out there and back."

"Then let's go. Sniffy can hold down the fort while I'm gone."

Which essentially meant that Sniffy would spend his time watching the drive and dodging those customers who didn't pump their own gas. He sniffed loudly in protest. He hated to be put on the spot.

"What if Beulah Peters comes in?" Sniffy said. "You know I hate that woman."

"She's already been in today, so you're in the clear," Danny said.

"What about Ruth?" Sniffy said to me. "She say anything about getting gas today?" Ruth also had Sniffy's number, and like Beulah, had been known to drag Sniffy out from the back room to pump her gas. It wasn't that she and Beulah couldn't fend for themselves, but the principal of the thing, since this was a full service station. That, and the fact each had a long running feud with Sniffy that dated from their high school days, and a long running feud with each other as well. It was a town and country thing between Beulah and Ruth, and who was where in the pecking order. More of a general nuisance thing between them and Sniffy. Mainly because of his loose lips and unwavering certitude, he got in people's hair long before he became a barber.

"She's at home cooking supper right now," I said. At least that was my fondest hope.

"I'm not getting off this stool unless it's an emergency," Sniffy said. "I'm not."

But Danny was already out the door.

Danny's pickup was a four wheel drive, silver-over-red, Ford 150. We could have taken his wrecker, but that would have been a waste of gas, and drawn more attention than I wanted. A wrecker run in Oakalla never went unnoticed, just as a fire run never went unnoticed. For good or ill, people here kept track of each other.

"So what are we after this time?" Danny said as we pulled into the drive there at the farm.

"A skeleton."

"I figured it was something like that."

"How so?"

"This isn't our first rodeo."

He had me there. "But maybe our last."

He stopped the pickup well short of the house. "What aren't you telling me, Garth?"

"I'm tired, that's all, of doing all the doing."

He shrugged and drove on. "Welcome to the club."

It wasn't until we had loaded the box in the back of the pickup and were headed back to town that he said, "You getting married have anything to do with what you said earlier?"

"Some. Not a lot. I'm about where you were a few months ago. Just tired of all the weight I'm carrying. I'd like to lighten my load a little."

"Good luck. That's all I can say. Once you put on your cape, it's hard to take it off."

"So we've learned the hard way."

Danny's smile spoke volumes. "Is there any other way, Garth?"

Then I noticed he was slowing down. "Is there something wrong with the truck?" I said. If so, and we needed help, the box in the back might be hard to explain.

"I think we have a tail."

"For how long?"

"Since we left the farm."

"A black pickup?"

"No. It looks more brown than black. And it might have something on the back. But it's too far away for me to tell."

"Large or small truck?"

"Small would be my guess."

"The one that followed me earlier looked large and black."

"You can turn around and see for yourself."

I turned around, but there was nobody behind us that I could see. "He must have turned off," I said.

"Yeah. He just did. Into the old Brainard mansion. Where to now?" We were coming into town.

"The shelter. We'll go in though the basement."

"You have a key?"

"That I do."

Chapter 2

"Most men bring flowers," Abby said with a smile.

"I'm not most men."

"How well I know."

Dr. Abby Airhart had straw blond hair that came to her shoulders, bright cornflower blue eyes, and peaches and cream skin that looked like it would never tan, but somehow did. She wore jeans and a pea green sweater, a small gold hoop in each ear, and a gold chain and locket that I had given her for Christmas a few years back. And black NIKE running shoes. We were standing in her basement, inside the morgue that had been built by her uncle, Dr. William Airhart, a world renown surgeon and pathologist, and a grand old man who had been murdered in his sleep that memorable year of snow on the roses. Abby and I were comfortable together. We had always been comfortable together from our first meeting on. On her return in January, I had expected some awkward moments, some painful silences, as we got to know each other again. There weren't any. It was as if she had never been away, as if that conversation that we had started at our first meeting had never ended. It almost seemed too easy, and I was leery of my happiness at first, while I waited for the other shoe to drop. It never did. I was starting to think that it never would.

"Any thoughts on the subject?" I said as we stared into the long wooden box that sat atop the slab there in the morgue.

"I'm thinking a white male somewhere in the prime of life." She used her tape to measure the skeleton. "Somewhere around five-ten or five-eleven. Stockily built, would be my guess."

"Any idea how long he's been in that box?"

She shook her head. "I'm good. But not that good. I'll have to run some tests."

"You don't have to tell me how good you are."

She blushed. She was a natural. "Don't take my mind off the subject. I still have a shelter to watch."

"Any clients at the moment?"

"Yes, I'm sorry to say."

But that's all she would say. Like Ruth, who watched the shelter in Abby's absence, she was closed mouth about the women who stayed there.

"That's too bad," I said.

"For a lot of reasons."

"Are you ever sorry you started the shelter?"

"Maybe on my worst days, when I find out things about people I'd rather not know."

"I know the feeling."

"I would imagine you do." I took her in my arms. She was easy to hold. "So what did you learn at the farm today?" she said.

"That I don't want to live there."

"Why not?"

13

"Because it doesn't feel like home."

She pulled away to look at me. "Neither does here."

"True. Not with the shelter here." The shelter had long been a bone of contention between Abby and me, and Ruth and me. I saw its need and applauded its work, but I could never learn to love it as I once did the house, before it became a shelter.

"What about Hattie Peeler's place? I hear it's for sale," she said.

"No. Hattie would haunt us for sure."

"You used to love that place. And Hattie as well."

"I used to love this place. And Doc Airhart as well. Time changes things."

"So what are we going to do?"

"I don't know. Let me think on it some more."

"Have you ever asked Ruth what she wants to do?"

"No."

"Why not? Is it because you are afraid of her answer?"

"Yes. Because I think I already know her answer."

"Sometimes you're very perceptive, Garth. Uncannily so. But you're not a mind reader. I'd ask her, if I were you."

"That's you're best advice?"

"That's my only advice."

I kissed her goodbye and started the walk home.

Now that the wind was calm, and the sky completely clear, the temperature had begun to fall, and I was no better dressed for the cold than I had been earlier in the day. We were well past sunset, deep into dusk, and as the sky faded from purple to black, I lingered a moment to watch it. Sunrise and sunset had always fascinated me, the way their colors ran from one moment to the next, especially if there were clouds present, and as tonight, if you weren't there at exactly the right moment, you missed the best of show. Sort of like Shakespeare's "tide," although with sunrise and sunset there were a host of second chances. But the point was not lost on me that you had to be there to see it, and could not be anywhere else.

Whoever had been following me earlier in the day was at least consistent. And persistent. He was back there again, somewhere in the shadows. But whether it was the near dark, or the situation, he seemed less a nuisance and more a menace than he had earlier. More malicious in his intent and more accomplished in his stalk, as if his mission had turned deadly. I had some knowledge of the subject. Over the past few years, I had been stalked by the best of them, experts and madmen alike. He seemed to fit somewhere in their midst. In fact, he might even be one of them.

Ruth seemed neither happy nor unhappy to see me, and barely acknowledged my arrival as I came into the kitchen. She was busy taking up supper, which included baked steak, browned potatoes, brown gravy, and canned corn. Not home canned corn right off the cob as in the past before she went to work at the shelter, but store bought canned corn that she doctored with pepper and butter into a reasonable facsimile. I had lost my tail outside the Corner Bar and Grill, just as soon as I stopped to wait under the street there on that corner. He seemed to melt into the night, which did nothing to reassure me about his intentions.

"You're late," Ruth said. "I was about to eat without you."

Ruth is a large, big-boned Swede who was still attractive in her seventies, but not the drop dead gorgeous blonde that she was as a younger woman. Her hair was long, and except for the gray roots, still mostly blond, but she usually wore it up, held in place with either a rubber band or a comb. She had never suffered fools as long as I had known her or been shy about voicing her opinion about anything, or anyone. Perhaps that was how we had survived over the years. Perhaps that's why I had hired her as my housekeeper in the first place. I liked straight shooters because I always knew where I stood with them. It was cheats, liars, and rationalizers that I couldn't abide. And equivocators. Who were perhaps the most tedious of all because I was sometimes among them.

"I have reason to be late," I said.

Over supper I told her my reason. As I sat there in my chair while she cleared the table, my belly full and my day unwound, I looked up at the round red clock with the yellow face and black numerals that had hung on the wall over the sink from my first day here, and felt a tinge of sadness that went all the way to my soul. It was going to be hard to give this up. Even for love.

"Why were you out at the farm in the first place?" Ruth said.

"Just looking around. I might want to live there sometime in the future."

"Why?"

"Just because."

"I wouldn't. Not for a million dollars. I had enough of farm life to last two lifetimes."

"Times are different now. There's not nearly as much work."

"So say you who never lived on one. And your summers with your grandmother don't count. She and the hired hands did all the work. You were just there to enjoy yourself."

I started to plead my case, but thought better of it. No sense digging a hole from which there was no escape. "You have any thoughts about the skeleton I found?" I said. "Abby says he was likely a white male in his prime."

"She's the expert. She ought to know."

"I'm asking what you think."

She stopped stacking dishes and turned to me with a sigh. "How many times have we been down this road, Garth, and what has it ever gotten us?"

"Some peace of mind."

"And a whole lot of grief."

Ruth and I were from two different camps. She believed that unless it was her ox that was being gored, it was better to leave well enough alone. I believed that the truth mattered, no matter whose ox was being gored, even if that meant sticking my nose into other people's business. Our positions had hardened over the years, and although she still would help me in a pinch, she only did so grudgingly. That was too bad because no one knew more about Oakalla and its people than Ruth.

The phone rang. It was Abby. "He's been dead somewhere between five and fifteen years," she said.

"You've already run your tests?"

"No. That's just a hunch. Besides, I know a guy who knows a guy."

"Is he there now?"

"He's on his way."

"Should I be jealous?"

"No." She hung up.

"Well?" Ruth said.

"I thought you weren't interested."

She went back to her dishes. "Suit yourself."

I told her what Abby had told me, and then about being followed from the farm and from the shelter.

"That changes things," she said. "The fly is already in the ointment."

"That's sort of what I thought. But who, Ruth? And why?"

"The who could be anybody. Lord knows you've stepped on enough toes over the years, and some of them are still walking around. But you find out the who, you'll know the why."

"Unless it's a whole new ballgame. Then the why comes first."

She put in the stopper and began running water. "And to think, I turned down Harvey Metzger to come live with you." Harvey Metzger was a retired farmer and a long time suitor who now lived in Arizona.

"But think of the fun we've had."

As she turned away, there were tears in her eyes. "I'm trying not to, Garth."

Chapter 3

It was a quiet cold Sunday morning in Oakalla. Nary a soul stirred as I walked the six blocks to my office there along Berry Street on the east side of town. I was reminded of my paper boy days back in Godfrey, Indiana, when my father and I and our white German shepherd would all pile into our Chevy Impala to deliver the Sunday Star. Queenie and I were in back, my father in front. He drove and folded. I delivered. Queenie barked and farted at the dogs and rabbits along the way.

There was something pristine about those early Sunday mornings, something inviolate. Especially when the cold crackled and the snow crunched. But it was the purity of fine glass, likely to shatter at the first sharp report. And something riotous and profane once the spell was broken. We laughed a lot those Sunday mornings, often at Queenie, more often at our own miscues. I missed them. And the man I called Pop, even more.

My office was in a flat roofed, one story, white concrete block building that housed the *Oakalla Reporter*. It never got really hot in there or icy cold, no matter what the season or the temperature outside. Its thick walls had something to do with that, its wide windows and baseboard heating the other. That is not to say that it was always comfortable in there, in particular mid spring and early fall when I couldn't decide whether I wanted the heat on or off or the windows open or closed. Usually I was too busy to worry about it until I noticed the sweat running or a chill setting in. This wasn't one of those times. I turned the heat up and put the coffee on before I went into the morgue to start reading.

I had an idea of that for which I was looking, but ten years worth is a lot of weekly papers to scour, even for someone practiced in the art. Neither could I skim them as I would have preferred to do because the article that I had in mind was not a headline grabber and might be buried anywhere in the paper. It was a relief, then, when the phone rang a couple hours later. My mind had started to wander, along with my attention to detail. I needed a break.

"Ryland here," I said.

"Airhart here," Abby said. "How goes it?"

"Slow. How about with you?"

"About the same. But there are a couple of things I wanted to tell you. First, healthy male likely in his prime is still in the ballpark, as is the time frame for his death. What both of us failed to notice, however, was the large hole in the back of his skull."

"How could we have missed that? Even at first glance."

"Easily enough done, since it's been filled in with plastic. An almost seamless job, I might add."

It took me a while to digest that. Then I said, "So, for sure, we're looking at murder."

"Not necessarily. He could have put a gun in his mouth and pulled the trigger, which from all indications is what happened."

"But not patched his skull up afterwards."

"No. That truly is a mystery."

"Anymore good news?" I said.

"He wasn't embalmed. But you probably already knew that."

"Which likely means there is no record of his death."

"I wouldn't think so. Well, I've got to run. Duty calls."

"Here or there?"

"There. I'm covering for someone at the hospital this afternoon."

"Watch your back," I said before she could hang up. "Someone followed me home from the shelter last evening. And from the farm yesterday afternoon."

"But not to the shelter?"

"I don't know about that. Why? What aren't you telling me?"

"Bright man that you are, I'm sure you'll figure it out."

I figured it out a moment after she hung up. If he hadn't followed me to the shelter, then he must have been in the neighborhood when I arrived. Which meant what? That he already knew ahead of time that I would be there? Or something else equally as puzzling?

At noon I walked to Corner Bar and Grill, sat at the bar, and ordered a fish sandwich and a draft of Leinenkugel's. The walk did me good. The sun was warm, the sky blue, the wind calm, the willows yellowing, the grass along Gas Line Road showing a hint of green. False spring or not, I'd take it, since spring itself was never a cake walk in Wisconsin.

"You want chips or fries?" Hiram, the bartender, said.

"Chips."

"Good. That's one less thing I have to cook."

"Where's all your help?"

"Look around the room, Garth. Who do you see?"

I'd already looked around the room and seen no one. "Are you saying it's a slow day?"

"That's why I sent my help home. Some Sundays are like that. But, as you well know, come Friday night, and you'll have to take a number."

Friday was "all you can eat" fish night and always packed as Hiram said. Monday-Saturday lunch hours were also busy and smoky and loud. And fun, as the regulars, mostly tradesmen and merchants, commiserated, as they swapped lies and gossip, and their heartfelt feelings about life in general. Sometimes things would heat up, especially over politics, but no blows were ever thrown. We all knew where everybody stood by now, and nothing short of death was going to change anyone's opinion.

While I waited for Hiram to cook my fish, I watched the Hamms bear log roll his way through yet another day. Although tastes in beer had changed mightily since that long ago moment when I first saw him skate across Grandmother's black-and-white TV screen, the Hamms bear would always mean Wisconsin to me.

"So what are you working on now?" Hiram said, as he set my fish and chips in front of me.

I already had my answer ready in case he asked because I wanted to give it as much circulation as possible, and this was the best place to start. Hiram could keep a secret with the best of them, but only if you asked him to.

"I'm doing a feature on the boys' basketball team, the one that went to the state."

"Which time? There were two, you know."

"The second one. I've already done the first one."

"Why now?" Hiram asked with his typical bluntness.

"It's the twentieth anniversary."

"Why not wait until twenty-five?"

"Because you never know," I said, and left it there.

That answer seemed to satisfy him. He went back to drying drying glasses, and I ate my lunch, took one last swallow of Leinenkugel's, and left.

It was mid afternoon before I found the article in question. That Larry Hanson was still missing was basically what it said. If anybody knew his whereabouts, he was to call Brooke Hanson at the number provided. Bingo! My instincts had been right along. I had my mission and I had my cover. Now, all I had to do was to sort it all out.

About a hundred yards up Gas Line Road, a figure appeared out of nowhere and quickly closed on me. I felt my heart start to race as I braced braced for the worst. Then I realized who it was and felt myself go limp in relief. I would live to fight another day.

"We've got to quit meeting like this," I said with a smile.

"How are you?" he asked.

"Not bad. How about yourself?"

"I can't complain. I'm back in school, thanks to you. I thought you might want to know."

Eighteen-year-old John White Bear had come into my life a few months back and left quite an impression. Smart, lithe, sinewy, and tough as nails, he was the most natural athlete I'd ever known, and one of the most accomplished.

Aside from the fact that he had saved me from a brutal beating, or worse, I liked him for his undaunted spirit and grace under fire. He liked me for reasons unknown. Had we been permitted the opportunity of growing up together, we likely would have become great friends.

"You running track this spring?" I said.

"Yes. The 1600 and the 3200. I figured why not, since I was there anyway."

"How's Andy doing?" Short for Adrianne (Bach).

A shadow briefly crossed his face, then moved on. "Fine, I guess. She's going to Smith College next fall."

"What about you?"

"I figure I'll probably go to a junior college around here. That's about all I can afford."

"You win the state in the 1600 or 3200, you can go about anywhere you want." Which he was fully capable of doing. In record time.

He smiled. It was priceless to see him smile because it was so rare. "Except Smith College. Besides, I don't want to make a living with my running, if you know what I mean."

"Expectations can get awfully heavy sometimes."

"That's what my uncle always says. 'It ain't no picnic being Chief.'"

"Your uncle is a wise man."

"So are you, Mr. Ryland. One of the very few I've met."

With that, he was off and running again. I watched him until he was a tiny dot that melted into the trees along Gas Line Road. "Godspeed, John White Bear. Godspeed."

Chapter 4

Keith and Cheri Miller lived in a brown stucco house two doors north of the shelter. Cant corner south across Madison Road was the vacant lot where the United Methodist Church used to stand until it burned a few years ago. We had built a new one west of town along Jackson Highway, and I had been there a few times, although not enough times to matter. What a church needed to survive was a minister who could preach, and who cared enough about his/her flock to see to their welfare, and a core of dedicated members intent on its well being. Although a church member, I wasn't part of its inner circle, but an outrigger attached to their mainsail. What I did best was to drag my feet, and insist that every proposed change have better than a good reason—a position neither popular nor(at first glance) defensible. But sometimes a contrarian is needed, even among the faithful, if only to keep them from giving the store away.

I was surprised when Cheri Miller answered my knock. I thought that she would be off somewhere doing her thing, which either involved community service or personal fitness. "Good afternoon, Garth," she said, as she stepped outside and closed the door behind her. That was my second surprise. Apparently she wanted to talk to me, which had never happened before.

"Is Keith around?" I said.

"No. I think he's at the gym, shooting baskets." She patted the porch swing whose rough, weathered slats matched the texture of house. "Sit. Please." It was more plea than invitation.

Cheri Miller was what my uncle Fred would have called "a handsome woman." Handsome didn't mean beautiful, or even feminine, but healthy, able, fit, and supple. Or in Cheri Miller's case, tall, tanned, stacked, and athletic. Although close to the same age, she and I would never be compatible. She was too public a person, too conscious a member of all the right organizations to suit me. I was too low on the social ladder to suit her. But that didn't mean that I didn't find her attractive, or that she wouldn't still be turning heads well into her next decade and beyond.

I sat down beside her on the swing. Neither of us spoke for a while, content to enjoy the warm sunshine that poured in from the west, and the utter calm of that Sunday afternoon. Meanwhile, she had leaned back and closed her eyes, as she let the sun have its way with her.

"You ever wish you were a kid again, Garth?" she said.

"About every other day."

"Same here. What I'd give to start all over again."

That seemed strange coming from a mother of four. "Without your children?"

Her eyes opened and she sat up in the swing. "Oh, we could be friends, and grow up together. They're all good people, everyone of them." And she would fight to the death anyone who said otherwise. "But they're about all out of the house. The last one graduates this spring." She turned her gaze on me. There was a heap of sadness in it. "So what am I to do, Garth, now that there's no family to hold together anymore?"

I gave her my best advice. "Be a kid again."

"I wish, but I think I've forgotten how. And sad to say, so have all of my friends. I have no playmates left."

"What about Keith?"

Her eyes snapped to life. "What about him? Besides the fact that he's a coward, liar, and cheat?"

She forgot adulterer, but maybe that was her definition of cheat. "Does he know how you feel?"

"He should. I've told him often enough. But he still wants my forgiveness. He still wants to work it out."

"And you?"

"I told you, Garth. I want to be a kid again. I want to start all over at ground zero. The only things that I want to bring from this life are my kids."

I didn't know what to say, so I didn't say anything, except to ask, "Why are you telling me all of this now? You wouldn't even give me the time of day before."

"That's because you never asked for it. And the reason I'm telling you this is because there is no one else to tell who knows the whole story from beginning to end, and yet has kept his silence. Which I'm asking you, please, to continue to do."

"I can do that. I've learned the knack."

"And I wanted to thank you for trying to save my marriage by making Keith do the right thing. It was way too late, that's all. She can have him now for all I care."

"I don't believe you."

"Okay. She can't. Not as long as he's sleeping in my bed."

I stood and brushed some paint flakes from my jeans. "You know hate and love are not opposites," I said.

"So I've heard. I don't believe it."

I wasn't sure that I believed it either, but it seemed the right thing to say under the circumstances. "Well, I'm off. You say Keith is in the gym?"

"That's where he said he would be. What do you want with him, if you don't mind my asking?"

I told her my cover story, which even I was starting to believe.

She raised her brows in question and then leaned back against the swing and closed her eyes. "Talk about a can of worms. Or more aptly, a den of vipers."

I asked her what she meant by that, but Cheri Miller was done talking for the day.

I stood outside the Oakalla High School gymnasium, listening to a basketball pound the hardwood inside. I knew the sound well. Long before March Madness was so named, and long before the mighty mites of Milan were immortalized in the movie *Hoosiers*, for even the average kid on the block, as I was, basketball was a way of life in Indiana. We ate it, drank it, talked it, dreamed it, and played it in all kinds of weather, and all times of day or night; and in every venue imaginable, including barns, bedrooms, and basements; and on concrete slabs and gravel driveways made into mud holes by recent rains or melting snow. But the inner sanctum, that Holy of Holies, was the high school gymnasium, even when we were practicing and playing there. Nothing made us happier than to sneak in there on a Sunday afternoon and play a pickup game against each other, or some of the older guys in town. You soon learned the pecking order and who had game and who didn't. And to wait your turn and to take your lumps without whining or crying about it. And when it was all over, when that gymnasium door forever closed behind you, almost always in defeat, you took along a bushel full of memories, some bitter, some sweet, that not even a lifetime of sharing, could empty.

When all went quiet inside, I banged on the door. "Keith, it's Garth Ryland. I'd like to talk to you."

I thought he might still be avoiding me until I heard footsteps coming my way. A moment later the door flew open with a bang. "About what?" he said.

I stepped inside and closed the door behind me before he could change his mind. "The twentieth anniversary of your state finals team."

"Give me a few minutes. I'm just about done." He went back to shooting baskets. I took off my shoes and rebounded for him.

Arnold Keith Miller was somewhere in his early fifties, stood about six three, and had a roundish face and body, gray-brown hair that was starting to thin, a small paunch that was starting to grow, and a short attention span, unless he was at the center of the conversation. He'd been a star basketball player for Oakalla, who in his senior year had led his team to the final game of the state finals where they lost in overtime by two points. He had a successful college basketball career at the University of Wisconsin, Whitewater, coached and taught at Phillips for a few years, then come back to Oakalla to coach basketball and teach math. He recently had concluded a successful twenty-two year run as coach and teacher and was now principal of Oakalla High School, where he hoped to remain until his retirement.

The last time I talked to Keith Miller was in late December at his office in the high school. He wore a coat and tie then, and a mustache that was too anemic to be taken seriously. Today he wore a plain gray T-shirt, red gym shorts, white athletic socks, black high top tennis shoes, concentration on his face, and sweat on his brow. And no mustache. I liked him a whole lot better this way. This seemed the real Keith Miller, not the caricature I had learned not to like. And he could still stroke it from well beyond the three point line, and I noticed that if he missed, he would make two in a row from that same spot before he moved on.

"Thanks, Garth," he said when he finished. "I can't remember the last time someone spotted me so well. You must have played the game once."

"A long time ago. But I was never nearly as good as you."

He shrugged. "Yeah, and look what it's gotten me. I'm a big fish in a small pond. Who isn't, if he has a little ability and plays his cards right? You should know. We're both in the same boat. The only difference is that you've learned to live with it, and yourself."

"Most days anyway," I said.

"I'd take one of those right about now."

He wiped himself off with a towel and we went to sit on the bleachers. Oakalla's gymnasium wasn't large compared to other high school gymnasiums. Its floor was regulation size, but there wasn't much room beyond that on either the sidelines or end lines. Just the perception of its low ceiling discouraged high arching shots, and ten rows of bleachers along either side of the floor were the most I had ever counted. Because of that, or because of something, sound carried in there about as well as in a bandbox. It hardly mattered when hundreds of partisans were shouting in my ear, but now, with just the two of us, I was too aware of the sound of my own voice, as I was with his. It seemed the whole town could hear what was being said.

"I just talked to John White Bear," I said to break the ice. "Thanks for letting him back in school."

"As if I had a choice."

"You had a choice. You made the right one."

"One of the few in my life. But that's not why you're here, I hope, to rub it in." If so, he was done talking.

"No. As I said, I'm here to talk basketball."

I was hoping he would take the bait. If not, it was going to be a wasted trip. To my relief, he said, "There aren't many of those guys left around here. Marcus Milner is about the only one. Unless you're counting managers. Then Tim Robinson would be your man."

Tim Robinson was now the janitor at the school. Or the maintenance superintendent, as he preferred to be called. Tim was sort of an odd duck who had never married and who had a fascination with all things basketball. He could quote time, place, teams, score off the top of his head from as far back as 1940, the date of the first NCAA basketball tournament now known as March Madness, to the present. And with the tournament due to start in four days, Tim would soon be in all of his glory, as he poured out statistics to whoever would listen.

"I'll talk to whoever I can, players, managers, coaches, cheerleaders, whatever. You all have stories to tell," I said.

"There's only one story to tell, Pug Hanson. All the rest of us were just along for the ride."

"What about Marcus Milner? Wasn't he the leading scorer?"

"Yes. He was a sophomore that year, Pug a senior. Pug got him the ball where he could do something with it, and he scored. It was as simple as that."

"What about the next two years when Pug wasn't there? Wasn't he the leading score then?"

"Oh, Marcus had talent. He was probably the most talented player I ever coached. Huge hands, and graceful as a gazelle. You see those guys palm basketballs on television, how they make it seem so easy? That was Marcus. But he made everything look easy. That was probably his downfall. Everything came so easily that he never took it seriously."

"And Pug?" He was on a roll. I wanted it to continue.

"Just the opposite. All guts and no glory, but without a doubt the best player I ever coached, and that includes my two sons, who were no slouches themselves. I mean Pug *willed* us to victory a lot of times. We won lots of games we never should have won because of him. Except that game in the semifinals against Abbotsford that we lost at the buzzer. That was ours for the taking, along with the state tournament. Do you know that Abbotsford beat Phillips by twenty points two nights later for the state championship? Twenty points! I get sick every time I think of it."

I had never seen Keith Miller so animated. It made me think that he might have a pulse after all. And help explain why two otherwise charming and accomplished women would waste their lives on him. "Why do you say it was yours for the taking?" I said. "Wasn't Abbotsford undefeated coming in? And ranked first in the state in Division 4?"

"So were we undefeated. And ranked third behind Sun Prairie, who we beat in the regional. That team had it all, Garth. We could score, defend, and rebound, but it all started with Pug Hanson."

"Then why did you lose?"

He didn't try to hide his anger. It still rankled him. "Picture this, Garth. We're up by two with seven seconds to go. We have the ball out of bounds at our end of the court along our sidelines because that's where they lost it out of bounds. Seven seconds, mind you. Our ball. We set a screen and Pug gets it into Marcus who's our best free throw shooter. But they don't try to foul him immediately and the seconds start ticking off. Now, all Marcus has to do is throw the goddamn ball down the court, and the game will be over by the time they retrieve it. But no, he's holding it back over his head, playing a cat and mouse game with the guy in front of him, while a guy sneaks up behind him, tips it away, grabs it, and throws a prayer at the basket just as the horn blows. I still think it was a tick too late, but no matter, the ref didn't see it that way, and the ball bangs off the bank board and goes in, and we lose by one. We go home, and two nights later they beat Phillips by twenty. Go figure, Garth. Two points ahead with seven seconds to go and the ball in the hands of our best free throw shooter. What are the odds of us losing that game in that way at that point? I've never gotten over it. I never will."

"It's hard to be philosophical about something like that."

"Damn near impossible. I was never at a loss for words after a tough game, but I was that night. When they needed me most, I had nothing to say. But maybe you can say it for me now in your article. I'm damn proud of them. Every one of them. They're the best team I ever coached, the best team Oakalla ever had."

"Even better than yours?" Keith Miller wasn't known for his humility.

"Way better, Garth. We couldn't have carried their jockstraps."

"So if he was that good, why didn't Pug go on to play college ball?" I said.

"Because he didn't want to play division III, who were the only ones showing an interest, and he didn't want to walk on at division I because he knew he'd never get a fair shot. Pug was five-ten, Garth, and not the fleetest of foot. There was no way to measure his heart. Whenever I think of Pug, I think of Scott Skiles. Pug didn't have quite his ability or his range, but he had his game. He was a winner. It's as simple as that."

"I'm glad you cleared that up," I said.

"You mean by not putting the blame on Brooke Childers?" (Who was later Pug's wife.) "She was part of it, sure. He didn't want to leave her here and him go away to maybe nothing. I mean, they had been together since fourth and fifth grade or so. But she wasn't all of it."

"Have you heard from Pug since he left town?"

"No. How long has that been, ten years now? I would have thought I would have heard something. It's not like we were strangers."

"He coached for you for a while, didn't he?"

"Not for me, although I offered him the job as varsity assistant. Girls JV. He was still coaching when he left. I've always wondered..." Then he waved that thought away.

"Wondered what, Keith?"

"I'm not really one to talk, Garth. Not with my history."

"I don't reveal my sources. You know that."

"Straight from the horse's mouth, isn't that how it goes? Oh, what the hell. The worst they can do is fire me. I've often thought that maybe he got his tit in a ringer with no way out. There was a girl on his basketball team that got pregnant and was making some noise that Pug might be the father. Either Pug or her boyfriend. That doesn't sit well in a small town, her being sixteen and him going on thirty. Especially not when you are in business for yourself. Then, of course, a year or so later, after the baby was born, she skipped town, too."

"I think I remember that."

He rose from the bleachers. "Of course, you do. You remember everything."

I put on my shoes, stood and offered my hand. He shook it. "Thanks, Keith. You've been a big help. And if you're still in touch with any of the guys, I'd like to have their names and phone numbers."

"I'm still in touch with most of them. I'll give you a call sometime tomorrow morning. On one condition. How did you find me here?"

"Cheri told me where you'd be."

"She wants a divorce, once our last kid is out of the house. She tell you that?"

"Not in so many words."

35

"Well, that's where we stand. Not that I blame her any."
Then he did something totally out of character. He drop
kicked the basketball all the way across the court.

"Feel better?" I said.

"Everything but my foot. I should have stayed in
coaching, Garth. Who needs the rest of this shit?"

"Apparently you did once upon a time."

"Thought I did anyway. X's and O's, Garth. When it's
all said and done, that's the only thing in life that counts.
Everything else is just marking time."

I couldn't argue with him. There was a lot to be said for
X's and O's. "Thanks again, Keith. Make sure you get those
names to me."

"I won't forget. And, Garth, forgive me for asking, but
where is your notebook?"

"I don't need one. As you said, I have a good memory."

"And I bet you never forget a slight either."

"No. Which brings me to my last question. Who took
over his team when Pug left?"

"Marcus did. He always seems to be following in Pug's
wake."

With nothing more to say, I left.

Chapter 5

Keith Miller was as good as his word. Shortly after I arrived at my office the next morning, he called to give me the names and phone numbers of the players and cheerleaders on the 20th anniversary team. I was surprised at one of the names there, but everything else seemed in order.

"Thanks, Keith," I said. "Just one one more thing. About what time does Tim Robinson get to the school?"

"Five on the dot. You can set your watch by him. He'll start in the grades and work his way toward the high school."

"He does both buildings by himself?"

"With time to spare. But don't get in his way or he'll run over you."

He hung up. Trying to choose my area codes wisely so as not to disturb any late risers, I began calling the names on the list. Almost to a man, they echoed what Keith Miller had said, that while Marcus Milner was its leading scorer and got most of the press, Pug Hanson was the team's heart and soul, the engine that drove the train. And each seemed comfortable with the part he had played, be it starter or reserve or afterthought, and had his own special memories from that season. But when asked whether theirs was the best Oakalla basketball team ever, each took the Fifth, unless it was off the record. They were less shy about proclaiming Pug Hanson the second best Oakalla player ever, right behind Keith Miller. There were no votes for Marcus Milner.

It was easy for them to talk about Pug Hanson the player, hard for them to talk about Pug Hanson the man. Few understood his decision not to go on to college, none his gradual cutting off all ties with them, or his sudden and complete disappearance. They were unanimous, though, in their opinion that he was still alive somewhere. They couldn't even imagine it being otherwise.

At noon I walked uptown to eat lunch at the Corner Bar and Grill and perhaps learn something more about Pug Hanson. It had gone from a cool, still, seamless blue morning to a warm and windy, partly cloudy day ahead of a cold front and showers due later that evening. "Nothing gold can stay" Frost wrote. That was particular true of Wisconsin in March. For every golden day, there were seven days of dross, with a couple of real stinkers thrown in.

Brooke (Childers) Hanson and Marcus Milner sometimes ate lunch together at the Corner Bar and Grill, occupying the last booth on the left in the dining room as you faced the swinging doors that led into the barroom. Following in her father's footsteps, Brooke Hanson was pharmacist at Childers Pharmacy and had been since Howard Childers leased the business to Wilmer Weimer and moved to Arizona several years ago. It had been Rexall Drugs from when I was a kid up until Howard Childers bought it and changed the name shortly after I moved to Oakalla. I once bought comic books and penny candy there. Now I bought bourbon and Advil. A lot more than that had changed over the years, but not its size and location there between the bank and the post office, or its main stock and trade, prescription drugs. People might be living longer than when I was a kid, but they didn't seem a whole lot healthier.

Compared to Brooke Childers, Marcus Milner almost seemed a Marcus come lately. He and his family had moved to Oakalla from Milwaukee his freshman year in high school, and his family had moved on to parts unknown his senior year of college. Marcus had stayed in Oakalla, renting a room from Beulah Peters while he went to law school at the University of Wisconsin, Madison. On graduation, he joined a law firm in Madison while continuing to rent from Beulah, and then had hung his shingle here after Maynard Wilson retired a couple years ago. From Beulah's he had moved in with Brooke Hanson, and her son, Howdy, and there he had stayed. Brooke Hanson was an only child. Marcus Milner had, I believed, a couple younger sisters. Aside from that, I didn't know much else about them except for their roles on the 20th anniversary basketball team, he as the leading scorer throughout the season and then the goat in their final game, and she, much to my surprise, as a varsity cheerleader.

I was in luck. Brooke and Marcus were dining out this Monday noon. "Do you mind?" I said, as I stopped beside their booth.

Each gave the other a questioning look. Sometimes I sat with others when all the booths and tables were full and there were no seats at the bar or the counter, but never with them. And today there were still a couple seat open at the counter.

"To what do we owe this honor?" Marcus said, as he scooted over to make room for me.

I thought Brooke would scoot over with him. But she held her ground, directly across from me. I couldn't quite judge the look on her face, but the nearest that I could come to it was pensive. Marcus, however, seemed pleased to see me, almost as if this were an everyday occurrence.

But that was Marcus Milner. Tall, lithe, and movie star handsome, he had a casual confidence about him that bordered on insolence—one of those people who are easy to like, but hard to embrace because you never know where they are coming from, or taking you. For a ride, or to the deep dark secrets of their soul? He reminded me a lot of Matthew McConaughey, at least the one I saw in the Lincoln commercials, and today in his jeans, sport coat, and white dress shirt open at the collar, he looked the part.

Marcus had asked the question, but Brooke Hanson seemed the one more intent on my answer. Tall, slender, forever pretty, sometimes attractive, with medium length, strawberry blond hair that curled up at the ends to rest on her shoulders, pale white skin that freckled instead of tanned, and emerald green eyes that rarely smiled, she usually looked pained about something, as if the water had just been shut off and the mortgage payment was overdue. Today was no exception. In her jeans and turtleneck, her head slightly bowed and her thin shoulders hunched, she appeared a schoolgirl back from the office after being rebuked for cheating on a test.

"I'm doing a feature story on Oakalla basketball, in particular your team that went to the state. I thought you both might have something to contribute."

"You're not wired, are you?" Marcus said. It was meant as a joke, but no one was smiling.

"No. And it's not on the record unless you say so."

"Who else have you talked to?"

"Coach Miller. Most of the rest of the guys."

"They tell you how I blew that last game, when we had it everything but won?"

"That was mentioned. Yes."

"I figured it would be. They've never forgiven me for that. None of them, including Coach Miller. You carry a team all season, and that's the thanks you get."

"You didn't carry the team all season," Brooke said with a fire in her eyes that I'd never seen before. "Larry did."

I was so used to everyone calling him Pug that it took a moment for it to register that he had a real first name.

"I stand corrected, Mrs. Hanson," Marcus said.

"Please don't call me that. I was only being fair."

Bernice, the owner of the Corner Bar and Grill, and its noontime waitress, came to take our orders. I, for one, was glad for the respite. There was no one more unwelcome than he who stepped right into the middle of a lovers' quarrel, which it appeared was what I had done. I ordered the special of the day—meat loaf with mashed potatoes and green beans on the side. It was a little heavy as my lunches went, but I was a sucker for their meatloaf and mashed potatoes.

"Let's start over," Marcus said with a smile after Bernice left. "Pug really was the star of that team. I, like everybody else, was just part of the ensemble. But it pisses me off not to get some of the credit. I mean somebody has to put the ball in the basket, and that somebody happened to be me. Not only that year, but the two years following. So let's give some credit where credit is due." Then he held up his hands. Keith Miller was right about their size. It was easy to see how he could palm a basketball. "But that's all off the record."

"Then give me something for the record."

"What do you want to know, how it feels to blow a game that means the state championship? Like eating a shit sandwich. That how it feels."

"I want to know about your basketball career after you left high school. I already know a little about your law career."

"Did you ask the other guys the same thing?"

"Yes. None of them had a basketball career after high school, unless you count coaching youth league."

That seemed to satisfy him. He said, "I was recruited by a couple Big Ten schools, Northwestern and Iowa, I believe, and invited to walk on at the U., but they all intended to make a shooting guard out of me, and I knew I was too slow for that. Or too lazy. You really have to work your ass off to get shots as a guard in the Big Ten, especially against guys that are taller and faster than you are. So I played at Wisconsin Green Bay for a couple years as a small forward, but never did crack the starting line up, so I quit. By then I was tired of it anyway. I never did have the love for basketball that Pug did, which was why I was never the player he was. The best high school player I ever played with or against. It was just a damn shame that he never went to college."

Had there been a way under the table at that moment, Brooke Hanson would have taken it. If Marcus Milner's intention was to make her feel small, he certainly accomplished his mission.

"Still, you coached girls' basketball here," I said.

"That was Pug's doing," he said. "He needed an assistant, so he talked me into it."

A thought crossed my mind, but I quickly dismissed it. I never liked jumping to conclusions because they were invariably wrong.

"Talk out loud," Brooke said.

I had to smile at her perception. Abby was always telling me the same thing. "I was just wondering about *your* thoughts on that season?" I said.

Her face softened. As always, I was struck by the change in her. When stripped of her perpetual frown, she was a thing of beauty. "Magical. The very best of times. There has been nothing in my life to match it, before or since." She shrugged. It was almost an afterthought. "Except the birth of my son."

"Ah yes, Howdy. Who could forget him?"

If looks could have killed, Marcus Milner would have been a dead man. "His name is *Howard*," Brooke said.

"Just like Pug's name is Larry, but everybody calls him Pug. Except you. It's not a crime, damn it."

Bernice brought a tray full of food and began handing it out. "And you've not heard anything from Larry since he left?" I said.

"No." She bit off the word.

"Not even to ask about your son?"

"He didn't know he had a son. I didn't even know I was pregnant at the time he left." She got up and dropped her napkin on her plate. "Excuse me, please." She left in the direction of the bar, which was also in the direction of the restrooms.

"IBS," Marcus said without concern. "It happens all the time."

"Have you heard anything from Pug?" I said.

"So now he's back to being Pug. But no, I haven't heard anything either. We weren't on the best of terms anyway, when he left. Emily Nelson was a good kid. At least until Pug got a hold of her."

"Is she the girl that Pug supposedly got pregnant?"

"Not supposedly, Garth. I see their kid in our house about every other night. He and Howdy are best buds. Where you see one, you're bound to see the other. But I wasn't talking about Pug's love life, which is none of my business. I mean he ruined Emily as a ballplayer. You can't talk to girls the way you do guys. Get in their face and yell at them. At least it never worked for me. Or on me when I was playing, which, to his credit, Coach Miller rarely did. But Pug wouldn't listen to me. There was only one way of doing things. His way."

"The fact that Emily was pregnant probably wouldn't help her on the court either."

"Point well taken, counselor. But I still think it went beyond that."

"And you think Pug is the father?" I said.

He had finished his sandwich. He took a long hungry look at Brooke's chicken salad before deciding against it. "Somebody is. Either Pug or her old boyfriend, who's not had any trouble having kids since."

I thought about asking his name, but now was not the time. I didn't want to appear too curious about someone who had nothing to with their basketball team. "Thanks,

Marcus," I said as I rose from the booth. "Please thank Brooke for me, too."

"I'll be sure to. And, Garth, really, how much of this is on the record?"

"Nothing that will get you in trouble with your clients."

"I'm not worried about my clients. I was thinking of Howdy and Billy."

"Billy?"

"Billy Nelson. Emily's boy. I think he might have game. Howdy, not so much, but he tries hard, just like his dad."

"Them either. This is a feel good story about a great basketball team. Nothing more, nothing less."

"I appreciate that. You go for the throat sometimes. I didn't want this to be one of those times."

I nodded, dropped a couple dollars beside my plate, paid for my lunch, and left.

Since I was in the neighborhood, I stopped by the Marathon on my way back to work. Already the clouds were starting to billow, and I could see a lone thunderhead far to the north, perhaps as far north as Lake Superior. Wind, waves, lightning bolts, and ice floes. What a great day for sailing, "on the big lake they called 'gitche gumee.'"

Danny Palmer was eating his lunch while ordering a part on his computer. Unlike me, he had mastered the beast and used it daily to his great advantage. I, however, had not, but knew my day of reckoning was close at hand because Abby had threatened to buy me one as her wedding present and fully intended to do so. And I couldn't very well keep it in my desk drawer, like the cell phone that she had bought me for Christmas.

"What's up, Garth?" Danny said. "Any progress on those bones you found?"

I looked around to make sure Sniffy wasn't there. Though cataracts had dimmed his sight, Sniffy had the hearing of an elephant. "A little. Do you happen to know Emily Nelson's old boyfriend's name?"

"What does that have to with anything? I thought you were doing a story on the basketball team."

"Who told you that?"

"I don't remember. But the word is out. Is it true?"

"Yes. That's my cover story."

"To get to whom?"

"I'd rather not say yet. Not until I know for sure."

"Fair enough. When will you know for sure?"

"When I find out to whom those bones belong."

"Back to my original question. What does Jared Cox have to do with it?"

"The same Jared Cox that's in here all the time?"

"He's a gear head, Garth. Where else would he be on his time off?"

Jared Cox was a rough carpenter who framed houses for a construction company located in the Dells. He also built race cars and raced them locally. He had a wife and three or four children, and a reputation for being a hard driver, but a good guy, neither overly aggressive or ambitious. Except for when he was in a race car, where he was hell on wheels.

"Thanks, Danny. That's all I wanted to know."

But he wasn't ready for me to leave yet. "Emily Nelson went missing, didn't she, Garth, about nine or ten years ago?"

"Yes. Nine years ago by my count."

"And you think those are her bones we found?"

"No." I left before he could pin me down. Danny might have a personal stake in this. He just didn't know it yet, as I didn't know what he might do about it.

Chapter 6

The clouds had been building and darkening all afternoon. Now, I could see lightning in the west and hear an occasional rumble of thunder. I glanced at my trusty Timex. Four fifty-five. I had been sitting on the grade school steps for ten minutes now. If Tim Robinson didn't show up soon, I was going get wet.

At exactly five p.m. a black Ford Ranger pulled up in front of the school, and Tim Robinson got out and began walking toward me. Tim wore short sleeve, navy blue coveralls, white socks, and black work shoes, and walked with a pronounced limp that seemed to worsen with every step. He quickly covered the remaining ground between us and had his key in the door before I could even say hello. I had to move fast to catch the door before it closed on me.

"Evening, Tim," I said as I followed him up the short steep flight of wooden steps that led to grades one, two, three, and four.

"Evening, Garth. Be with you in a minute."

Wound is the best way to describe Tim Robinson. Taut, lean, and wiry, "not an ounce of fat on him," as Grandmother would have said, he stood about five-nine with G.I. short, white-blond hair, piercing gray-green eyes, a sharp narrow face, and no sense of humor. I'd tried in the past to get him to smile and show me his lighter side with absolutely no luck. With Tim, what you saw was what you got, which was a lemon sucker who spent his life at fast forward. We would never be friends, but I did respect his honesty and his work ethic that ended at the schoolhouse door. Once away from there, his time was all his own, and he could be as frivolous as the rest of us.

He went to the first floor closet, got his dust mop and trash can on wheels, and started for the first grade classroom. If I didn't detour him soon, I could already see how my night would go, as I chased him from room to room, trying to get a word in edgewise.

"Pug Hanson," I said.

He stopped dead in his tracks. "What?"

"Pug Hanson. Was he as as good as everyone says he was?"

"Probably better." He started to move on, then changed his mind. "Why do you want to know?"

"I'm doing a story on that team, and talking to all of its members." He didn't have to be told what team. He knew its history far better than I.

"I wasn't on that team, remember. I was manager."

"Yes, you were. All the way from fifth grade up until you broke your leg your sophomore year. You and Pug were paired at guard."

Taken by surprise, he sat down with a thump on the stairs that led up to grades five and six. It pays to do one's homework.

"I never told you that," he said.

"I have other sources." Old newspapers in particular. Theirs was a special class of athletes. They never had a losing season at any level at any sport and won several championships along the way.

"Did your source tell you that Pug was the one who broke my leg?"

"No."

"Not that he did it on purpose," he was quick to add. "We were playing a game of two-on-two against each other in practice. You know, where the winners stay on the court and the losers sit down. Coach liked to pit Pug and me against each other because if we were teammates, we'd hardly ever lose. Well, Pug and his partner had been out there forever, and I was tired of losing to him, so when I beat Pug on a crossover and started for the basket, I was determined to score come what may. Pug had other ideas. He caught me in mid jump and laid me out, never trying to block my shot. I landed wrong, and the next thing I knew there was blood everywhere and the bone was sticking out of my leg." He was so matter of fact, he might have been talking about a jammed finger.

"I'm sorry, Tim. I know how good you were up until then."

"But never as good as Pug. Although I do think I was the better all around athlete. Just not on the basketball court."

"Did his last game go down the way everybody said it did?"

"How? Swivel hips playing a game of chicken with the ball? You're damn right it did. What a showboat! I've never forgiven him for that. The ball should have been..." He held them out to show me. "In these hands. Not God himself could have stripped it." He sighed as he got up. "But that's all in the past, Garth. Water over the bridge."

"Have you heard from Pug since he left town?" I said before he could get away.

"Not a word. We used to be best friends. Long time ago. Before he stole my girlfriend."

"Who was that?"

"Guess."

"Brooke Childers."

"Good guess." Then he was off to work.

I waited for the rain to change to a drizzle before starting for home. It had become night in the interim, the storm abetting the darkness, its low clouds one with the earth. With every streetlight came a white halo of fog that rose ghost like to meet me, then fell in my wake. On such a night as this, with workday done and supper on the stove, I thought I would have the streets of Oakalla to myself. I didn't. Someone was back there following me. I couldn't see him, but I felt his presence, and it gave me the willies. Then, a block from home, he went away. I could feel his shadow lift as surely as I felt my spirits rise. Ally, ally out, I was home free.

Ruth was in the kitchen cooking supper. I left my shoes at the front door and went upstairs for a hot shower and a change of clothes. When I came down again, supper was on the table. Ham steak and gravy, fried potatoes, and mustard greens by the looks of it. It felt good there in the kitchen with the lights bright and the food steaming and the heat from the stove settling in. I was going to miss the meals almost as much as the house. Not that Abby couldn't cook, but because of the hours she worked between the university and the hospital, she rarely did. Not that I couldn't cook. I just didn't want to. But better I didn't think about that.

"If I throw some names at you, will you give your first thoughts about them?" I said.

"Why?"

"Because you know more about this town and its people that anybody else, and I need some honest answers from someone who has no dog in the fight."

"To what purpose?"

"Just humor me, please. For old times sake."

"Neither of us is dying, Garth. Just going our separate ways."

She hit the nail on the head. It really did feel like a death in the family.

"Where's Daisy?" I said. Daisy was Abby's English setter that we had kept while Abby was away. She should have been in the kitchen with us, her paw on Ruth's lap, begging for food. Ruth, who in all of her years on the farm wouldn't even let an animal in the house, let alone the kitchen.

"I took her to the shelter with me this morning and left her there. She's Abby's dog, Garth. They need to get reacquainted."

"Was Abby back when you left?"

"Just walking in the door."

"Good," I said. "They can keep each other company."

"That's what I figured. Now, about those names..."

"Pug Hanson," I said.

"The second best basketball player to ever play here."

"Keith Miller being the first?"

"Yes." As much as she hated to admit it.

"What about Pug Hanson the man?"

"You knew him as well as I did, Garth. What do you think?"

"What I think doesn't matter. That's why I'm asking you."

"Certainly not a happy man. At least he didn't seem to be."

"What about the rumors?"

"That he fathered Emily Nelson's child? Who knows what, under the wrong circumstances, any of us will do?"

"Brooke Childers Hanson," I said.

"Pretty girl. Unhappy woman. She never really had a chance. But I think she's very good at what she does."

"What do you mean by not having a chance?"

"Who else was going to marry Pug Hanson, run the drug store after her dad left? They had it all planned out for her. Somebody did anyway."

"Maybe she planned it herself."

"Maybe she did. Whoever's to blame, it turned out to be a bad bargain. She's stuck here, probably for the rest of her life."

"Some of us like it here," I said.

"And some of us fit here, and some of us don't. I don't think she does anymore."

"What about Marcus Milner, does he fit here?"

"Here and nowhere. One place is as good as another to him."

"Or as bad?"

"It's all the same to him. Life's a game, that's all, nothing to be taken seriously."

"How do you know so much about him?"

"I watched him play basketball a few times. That's all it took. And watched him in court when I was on the jury last year. He's lazy, Garth, when it comes right down to it. But he has so much God given ability no one would ever know."

"Tim Robinson," I said.

"Man on a mission. He just doesn't know what his mission is half the time."

"He cleans the whole school by himself."

"So could I have, back in the day. And then cooked supper, done the dishes, and put the kids to bed. Because he's always so intent on what he's doing, it's hard to find fault. But anybody who spends all his free time memorizing basketball scores has got a screw loose somewhere. In my book anyway."

My list was narrowing. I had only one name left. "Barbara Hanson." Who was Pug Hanson's mother and my next contact.

"Tight lipped as they come. You'll be lucky to get a word out of her."

"She used to talk to me."

"And how long ago was that?"

I had to think about it. "You're right, Ruth. It's been about ten years or so. I don't remember seeing her in the Corner since Pug left town."

We had finished supper. But Ruth had yet to start clearing the table, and woe to me if I started ahead of her. She knew exactly where she wanted every pot, pan, glass, plate, serving spoon, and eating utensil, and would brook no deviance from that arrangement.

"Did Pug leave town?" she said.

"No. I don't think so."

"That's what I was afraid of. When will you know for sure?"

"Whenever I can get Abby a sample of his DNA."

"How are you going to do that?"

"I don't know yet. I'm hoping the answer will reveal itself."

"Knowing you, I'm sure it will."

She began clearing the table. I went to the phone and called Abby at the shelter.

"Good evening, Mr. Ryland." I loved the sound of her voice. It was music itself.

"Good evening, Dr. Airhart. Are you alone?"

"Except for Daisy. My house guest left early this morning. Why? What are your intentions?"

"Not honorable, I assure you."

"I was hoping you'd say that. How soon can you be here?"

"I'm on my way now."

"Good."

I hung up and said to Ruth, "I'm on my way to the shelter. It might be late before I get home."

Her back was to me. She didn't say anything.

"Did you here me, Ruth?"

"You're a grown man, Garth. You don't need my permission."

True, although I sometimes felt as though I did. "I wasn't asking permission. Just stating facts."

"Then turn the porch light on when you go."

I said I would, grabbed my watch cap and fleece jacket out of the hall closet, and left.

Chapter 7

It was a cold walk to work the next morning, the cold made all the sharper by my lack of sleep. But it was worth every step of it. I only wished I'd made it home as I told Ruth I would.

Abby had nothing more to add concerning the skeleton I'd found. Except for one thing. Two things, actually. She was becoming more and more convinced that the wound was self inflicted, or at least made so it appeared to be. She also said that two of the metatarsal bones on the feet had been switched, from left foot to right foot and right foot to left, which indicated that the skeleton had been reassembled at one point. She also had found bits of clothing on the skeleton, although there was no clothing as such in the box, which told her that the body had been clothed at the time of death and also gave further proof that it had been moved at least once before being moved to Grandmother's root cellar. But as far as age and condition of health at the time of death, nothing had changed. Unless I wanted to count an often sprained right ankle.

The day began with a light breeze and a clear blue sky, but soon the clouds started to roll in, and by noon it was cloudy, blustery, and growing colder by the minute, as the wind cut through my fleece jacket on my short walk to Barbara Hanson's house. However, after my phone call home to tell Ruth that I was okay, the day seemed warm by comparison.

Barbara Hanson lived a block south of my office at the intersection of Berry and Center streets. Her front porch faced west, and Berry Street. Her garage faced north, and Center Street. Two large silver maples grew along Berry Street in front of the house, and the rest of the house was shaded by an assortment of pines and hardwoods that grew in the yard and the easement beyond. The house was wooden, painted a forest service green, with wooden front porch steps, black shutters, and a black shingle roof and two dormers that looked out on Berry Street. Barbara's Maroon Chevrolet Impala was parked in the driveway that led to the garage, and beside the garage, in the easement that was once an alley, was a large, leaf-covered camper that belonged to George Peterson, Barbara's live in companion. Or boyfriend, depending on one's point of view. Once a man and a relationship reached a certain age, I had a hard time calling him a boyfriend. Or significant other, which covered all bases, including the family dog.

Barbara Hanson had worked second shift, three to eleven, at Capital Plastics in Madison for as long as I had known her. Capital Plastics had gotten its start during World War II making plastic toy soldiers and other cheap plastic toys. Now, they made mostly pill bottles and other pharmaceutical containers. Barbara had gone from line worker to supervisor, back to line worker, and that's where she'd stayed. If she was happy about anything, she was happy about her job, which provided a good income with minimum stress. The hours were a "bitch" at first, she had said, but not bad once you got used to them. The only bad part was that she missed most of Pug's basketball games.

She must have seen me coming. She opened the front door before I could ever knock.

"I gave already," she said.

"And a good afternoon to you, too, Barbara."

Barbara Hanson was small and thin with short gray hair, hazel eyes, a hard mouth, and a slightly crooked nose that gave her the look of the combatant she was. She said her former husband had broken her nose in one of their many fights before she booted him out and moved to Oakalla when Pug was in kindergarten; or at least not yet in first grade because he had started school here. She said of her former husband that he was a good man, but a mean drunk, and while she could happily live with the one, she couldn't the other. And although life had been hard at times, she had no regrets.

"If you don't mind," she said, as she pulled a cigarette from her flannel shirt pocket and lighted it. "I'm trying to quit because my doctor says it's killing me. But slowing down is the best I can do."

"Until when?"

"It kills me, I reckon. My problem is, I like to smoke. Always have, always will."

"Even if it kills you."

She shrugged. "We all have to die from something, Garth. Where have you been these past few years? I've missed you. One of the few people in this town I can say that about."

"Where have you been? That's the question."

"Everywhere I used to be. Except not nearly as often. Everywhere except the Corner Bar and Grill and a couple other places where I no longer feel welcome."

"If you hate Oakalla so, why don't you move to a happier place? You have the money."

"Also my reasons for staying here. Now, before you give me any song and dance, I know why you're here, and the answer is no."

"How can you know why I'm here?"

"George has his ear to the ground at all times. He said to expect you."

"Be sure to thank him for me. On second thought, I'll do it myself."

"Be my guest. He'll be at work all day. And you know George. He's hard to miss." Especially at five-eight and two-fifty or so.

"Why won't you talk to me about Pug?"

"Like I said, I have my reasons. And his name was Larry. He hated the name Pug. He said it made him sound like one of those squeaky little lap dogs."

"That's what Brooke calls him, Larry," I said to see her reaction.

"I know," she said sadly. "That's one of the few things that girl and I ever agreed on. Now, if you will excuse me..." She started to close the door on me.

"You said his name *was* Larry. That's in the past tense."

"I know," she said, then stepped inside and closed the door.

George Peterson was a former long distance trucker who was now a taxidermist, operating his business out of the building that stood west across School Street from the Corner Bar and Grill, and that used to be the post office way back when. He also owned what was once the Standard Service Station next door along Jackson Highway, but used that building mainly for storage. Thick and squat with coarse, black hair and a salt and pepper beard, he was never without two things, his tinted sun glasses and red baseball cap. I liked the man. He was easy to talk to and a good listener, but I couldn't say I knew him well. An orphan, raised in a foster home, he seemed to have a chip on his shoulder that was not directed at any one person, but life in general. He felt that he had been dealt a bum hand as a kid and had never quite gotten over being odd man out. So he was prickly without appearing so, a porcupine dressed as a teddy bear.

George's taxidermy shop smelled like an ill-kept meat locker inside. I knew that going in, which is why I went there before, instead of after, eating lunch at the Corner Bar and Grill. Better to lose my appetite than my lunch. George was wearing bib overalls over a red-and-black plaid flannel shirt and polishing the antlers of a twelve point buck. It was an impressive set of horns. Maybe not a Boone & Crockett, but close.

"Nice rack," I said. "Where did it come from?"

"Some guy from the Rapids. I'm trying to get caught up before fishing season starts."

I fought the urge to take off my jacket and hang it outside. The smell in there wasn't overwhelming, but very dense and pervasive, like that of skunk once the dust settles.

"So what brings you here in the middle of the day?" George said.

"As if you didn't know. I thought we were friends."

He feigned ignorance, something at which he was good. "I don't know what you're talking about."

I wished I could see into his eyes just once to better judge his state of mind. But those tinted glasses always kept me at bay. "You called Barbara to warn her off before I even had a chance to plead my case."

He shrugged. "She wouldn't have talked to you anyway. Not about Larry. I thought I might as well save you both time."

"Why won't she talk about Larry? He's been gone ten years."

"It's what went before, according to her. I was new in town then. Barb and I were just getting acquainted, if you know what I mean. There were rumors going around about him that she didn't like. Not only didn't like, but set her teeth on edge. She thought people should have come to Larry's defense, after they once had carried him so high. But they didn't. And she never forgave them. Them or this town either one."

"Then why does she stay here?"

"That's what I keep asking her. You've seen that camper out behind her house. Five years old and it's still almost brand new for all of the miles we've put on it. I told her we could go anywhere in the country and just camp out along the way. Live in the mountains in summer and the desert in winter and somewhere else in between. But I can't even get her out of the house on the weekend. I go myself sometimes, in my little Toyota and shell, to some of the state parks around here, but that gets old after a while. Being by myself, I mean. I had enough of that on the road, which was the main reason why I sold my rig. Of course, if I knew how much work this was going to be, I might have taken up something else in my spare time."

"I sometimes feel the same way, George. Except I love what I do."

"And I love her, which is why I keep hanging around. But it does get old after a while. Not going anywhere, I mean."

I knew what he meant. As a young man, I had traveled the country, eagerly and often. I thought I might like to do it again someday. Before I got too old.

"You knew Larry, if only briefly. Did you put any stock in those rumors?" I said.

"No comment, Garth."

"On the grounds it might incriminate you?"

"I said no comment. Larry and I didn't see eye to eye on much of anything from the time I first started seeing his mother. I think most of it was the fact that he'd had her to himself all those years and then he didn't."

"And the rest of it?"

"He thought I was after her money. True, she did loan me the money to buy this place. But I've long since paid her back. It took selling my rig to do it, but I did." And now I'm stuck, he could have said, but didn't.

"Anymore thoughts on the subject?" I said.

"No." He laid down his buffing rag and walked over to a sink to wash his hands. Made of stainless steel, the sink was large and deep enough for him to have taken a bath in there had he wanted. "I'd help you if I could, Garth. But I can't. Not where Larry is concerned."

"I notice you call him Larry, not Pug," I said.

"Years of practice, Garth, years of practice. You learn to make some mistakes only once."

I left George ruminating on that thought, while chewing on one of my own. "Of all the sad words of men or pen, the saddest are these, it might have been." As I stepped outside, the sky suddenly darkened, and it began to spit snow. Perfect. Just perfect.

After lunch, I spent the rest of the afternoon working on that week's edition of the *Reporter*. But most of my sources and advertisers were more interested in talking basketball than the usual business at hand. After a while, I gave up trying to steer them in my direction and went with the flow. If they wanted to talk basketball, we would talk basketball, and the paper be damned. Except I was taking notes the whole time to make sure that not only did I get my quotes right, but that I didn't leave anybody out. Hell hath no fury like a source scorned, especially when it came to basketball. I blamed the University of Wisconsin at Madison for that. Had it been content to be a cellar dweller in either football or basketball, the people of Oakalla might not now be so spoiled, or so partisan. But after all the noise it had made on the national stage lately, sports fever ran high, along with expectations. There was no such thing as a quiet Saturday in fall anymore than there was a quiet Saturday in March. As long as the Badgers were on a roll, Oakalla was rolling with them. And as much as Ruth might long for the good old days when her Packers were the only show in town, even she had to admit it was a fun ride.

It had started to clear when I glanced out my office window shortly after five. What clouds there were had a pink hue to them, and the sky a pastel blue somewhere between robin's egg and Rocky Mountain high. But by the time I reached Barbara Hanson's front porch, it was the color of nightshade.

I climbed the porch steps and knocked on the front door. I wished the steps and porch had been anything but wooden because each crack, creak, and groan made me too aware of my mission. I knew Barbara would be at work, and I was sure that George would still be uptown tipping a couple before supper at the Corner Bar and Grill. But I knocked anyway before I tried the door, which, not surprisingly, was unlocked.

I didn't know exactly what I was looking for, just that I'd recognize it when I saw it. It was dim inside the house and getting dimmer by the second, but I hadn't thought to bring a flashlight and didn't have the guts to turn on a light. It was a shock, then, when a light in the living room came on. I was about to raise my hands in surrender when I realized that the light had been tripped by a timer. I knew some people around town had them for security purposes, but it never dawned on me that Barbara Hanson would be one of them, especially with the hulking presence of George Peterson around.

With the fat in the fire, I didn't have time to take inventory. I went to the nearest closet and started pulling hangars. At the time of my father's death, which closely followed that of my mother, I was surprised at how much of me was still around when my sister and I started cleaning house. Along with games, toys, letters, and track ribbons, there were basketballs, baseballs, and footballs, and clothes I hadn't worn since high school. There had to be something of Pug Hanson here. My hope was that it would be within easy reach. As it turned out, it was. At the back of the closet, just as my legs had started to turn to jelly, I found his old letter jacket. On any occasion it would be a prize worth keeping. Tonight it was a godsend.

I left the way I'd come and headed for the shelter. Little time had passed since I first entered the house, but it seemed longer. Much longer. The night agreed, as darkness fell quickly, along with the temperature. But I didn't feel my tail behind me, as I hadn't felt him the night before on my way to the shelter—not since he had abandoned me a block from home. It seemed that I'd passed some sort of test, and he was no longer interested in me. That was good because I didn't want to drag Abby into this any further than I already had. We had been too long in the making for me to lose her now.

"You realize that we can't use this as evidence if it ever comes to trial," Abby said, as she blotted the jacket with masking tape, searching for hairs.

"It won't come to trial, not if you're right about it being a suicide," I said.

"Still..."

"Come on, Abby. Now you're starting to sound like Ruth." That was a mistake. Thick, dead silence followed, the kind you can cut with a knife and serve on a plate.

"If you don't want my help, just say so," she finally said.

"I'm sorry. That was uncalled for. But it's been a long day."

"For both of us."

"How so?"

"Sometimes I don't think I'm cut out to be a teacher. At least to students who want a grade, but don't want to learn. The times that I'm happiest and at my best are at the hospital—in the emergency room of all places. Life has an urgency there that it doesn't have anywhere else."

"That's because it's life and death. As the old song goes, you can't have one without the other, not if you like living on the edge."

"I never thought I'd turn out to be that kind of person, an adrenaline junkie, but it appears I am. I just don't know what to do about it without turning my apple cart upside down again."

I could feel a knot start to grow in my stomach that, if not checked, would soon be the size of a softball. We had a similar conversation right before she left Oakalla with no thoughts of returning.

She correctly interpreted my silence for what it was because she then said, "But I'm not leaving you again. That's a given."

"You know you can work the emergency room full time," I said. "They need surgeons as much as anyone."

"More than anyone, Garth. Some nights you can't believe the carnage, what we do to each other with our knives, guns, and automobiles. It's all I can do to stop the bleeding."

"At which you're very good. Don't ever forget that. And as another old song goes, every form of refuge has its price."

"So what about the past three years? Do I just chuck that?"

"Just answer me one question. Would you rather work on live people or dead ones?"

Her smile gave her away.

"Then you have your answer," I said.

"You won't care if I don't keep a regular schedule?" she said.

"The only thing I care about is you."

She gave me a great big hug. I hoped we didn't ruin our DNA sample and have to start all over. But then I noticed the masking tape was still on the jacket.

It was time for me to go. Supper would soon be on the table, and with Ruth on the warpath, I didn't dare be late.

"How soon will you know anything?" I said, taking the jacket with me. With any luck, I'd have it back in the closet at this time tomorrow.

"A day or so, maybe longer. It depends on how many arms I have to twist."

"You can't do the tests yourself?"

"No. I'm not certified."

"Let me know as soon as you can then."

"Why the rush... after ten years?"

"Because that skeleton hasn't been in my root cellar for ten years, or even ten weeks. Something's afoot. I just don't know what."

"Do you think you're sitting on a powder keg?"

"Yes. And I think I already lit the fuse." I put my arms around her. She was easy to hold. "But don't worry. I've been here before."

"Words of comfort to your beloved, I'm sure." She rested her head on my shoulder. "I just realized something about us. We both like living on the edge."

"You so more than I," I said. "I'm just an accidental tourist."

"You could have fooled me."

Both of us, had I been completely honest. But I was tired of the balancing act. I no longer climbed on roofs either, if I could help it. At some point in time you just know when enough is enough. It's not a matter of strength or of courage, but of will. You can't make yourself take that further step because in your gut you know it might be on air.

"Where to now?" she said.

"Home, and supper."

"And after that?"

"Bed. As I said, it's been a long day."

"That's because it was a short night."

"How could I forget?"

I kissed her and left.

Chapter 8

The phone rang early the next morning while I was downstairs making coffee. Ruth had yet to arise. I had yet get my wits about me. At five past six, it must be important.

"Hello," I said, my voice still husky from sleep.

"Garth, if that's you, I want Larry's letter jacket back here within the hour."

There was no sense asking who it was. It could only be Barbara Hanson. But how could she know that I had the letter jacket? No matter. She did. "Will do," I said.

"Then you don't deny it?"

"There's nothing to deny. You caught me red handed."

"I ought to call the law," she said.

"I am the law in Oakalla. Such as it is."

"Tell me another one."

"I'll show you my badge when I get there."

That gave her pause. I'd just taken the wind out of her sails. "You still had no right," she said.

"Agreed. That's why I'm returning it."

"Then see that you do," she said, and hung up. Or hit the off button on her cell phone. One never knew these days.

Meanwhile Ruth had come into the kitchen and poured us each a cup of coffee. She wore the faded flowered robe that I had given her one Christmas years before and that she refused to part with, even now that it had started to fray. She looked about as I felt—hung over and dog tired. And to think, we fancied ourselves morning people.

"Who was that?"

"Barbara Hanson. She wants Pug's letter jacket back within the hour."

She yawned. "I didn't know you had it."

"I didn't, until last evening."

She put some cream and sugar in her coffee and scooted them across the table to me. "It seems you're up to your old tricks again."

We had made peace over supper last evening. I hoped it wasn't about to be broken. "Sometimes I can't help myself, Ruth."

"How well I know." She had her opening, but to my relief, didn't take it further.

"What I don't understand, is how she knew," I said. "I'm sure nobody saw me."

She took a drink of her coffee. "Have you ever heard of security cameras, Garth?"

"Yes, but why would she need one with George around? She has her lights on timers, too."

"Says he who is hiding the bones of her dead son."

"By his own hand, Abby thinks."

"That's beside the point, and you know it."

"No, I don't. You don't rig up security cameras and lights on timers unless you feel threatened. At least not in Oakalla."

"Which has never had any bones show up until now. Come on, Garth. Stop kidding yourself."

"I guess I'm living in the past," I said.

"It wouldn't be the first time."

"But I still don't think I'm wrong."

"What makes you so sure?"

"You said it yourself, Ruth. The bones of her dead son."

"If they're his." She still wasn't convinced. But that was nothing new. The last time anyone had won an argument with Ruth, FDR was president.

I shaved, took a quick shower, and headed for the east end of town. The sun was not yet up, but the morning showed promise with Venus bright and twinkling in an otherwise empty sky. I had always liked mornings, especially first light. At sunrise the day belonged to everyone else, but that time between dusk and daylight was all mine.

Barbara Hanson stood at her front door waiting for me. I didn't even have to knock. But before she could say anything, I took out my wallet and showed her my Special Deputy badge. If she was impressed, she did a good job of hiding it.

"Just tell me why," she said as I handed her the jacket.

"If you'll do the same."

"Why what?" she said.

I pointed to the camera overhead, the one I had failed to see last evening. "Why the security cameras? And why won't you talk to me about Larry?"

"Like I said, I have my reasons."

"Well, so do, I Barbara. Have a good life."

"That's all you have to say for yourself, have a good life? So you're writing me off, too, just like you did Larry?"

"I never wrote him off. That's why I'm here now. You're the one who's written him off, the one who won't talk about him."

"And you're the one who stole his letter jacket. What did you plan to do with it, give it back to her?" 'Her' could only mean Brooke Hanson. But before I could deny it, she said, "She wanted it, you know. But I wouldn't give it to her."

"Before or after Pug left? *Larry* left."

"After. She said she wanted it for his son. But I wouldn't let go of it, which is why he has yet to darken my door. And I'll tell you one more thing, Garth. Everybody says Larry is the one who didn't want to go on to school, when the truth is, she was the one who didn't want him to go on to school. She was after him to get married from the time he graduated high school up until the day they did get married."

"Which was when?"

"At the end of her sophomore year in college. He's the one who put her through pharmacy school, despite all that 'poor me' on her part and that of her big talking father. With his own two blue collar hands—for all of the good it did him."

"Why did they get married then? I mean at that particular time, if you don't mind my asking?"

"She was pregnant. Or said she was anyway. But either she lost the child or she was lying to him, one or the other."

"And you never see your grandson?"

"Not if she can help it."

"There is such a thing as grandparents' rights. I'm sure it would apply in your case."

"Why bother, Garth? He's got legs. He knows who I am and where I live."

She had a point, albeit a weak one. Kids instinctively knew where they were welcome and where they were not. Thinking I had gotten all that I was going to get, which was way more that I expected, I decided to leave before she realized I had never answered her question about the letter jacket. Neither did I intend to. I got as far as the bottom step before she yelled at me.

"Garth?"

"Yes, Barbara?"

"That's all on the record if you want it to be."

I nodded, just to appease her. Over my dead body.

"I mean it, Garth. I've got nothing nothing to hide. Unlike some other people I know."

I had to bite my tongue to keep from asking whom. Although she didn't know it yet, Barbara Hanson was part way into my camp. I didn't want to scare her off by appearing too eager, by asking a question she would then refuse to answer. This was a fishing expedition on her part to gauge my motives. I didn't take the bait.

"I'll take that into consideration," I said, and went on to work.

Most of the rest of the morning was spent taking phone calls, until finally I had to take the receiver off the hook to get any work done. Word had gotten out about my story and everyone in town, it seemed, had an opinion about that magical year, including those who had since moved here, or had since moved away. Twenty years didn't seem like all that long a time span until I put it in perspective. The Great Depression, World War II, the Berlin Airlift, and Korea would all fit into that time frame, as would the

Cuban Missile Crisis, the assassinations of John Kennedy, Robert Kennedy, and Martin Luther King, Jr., Vietnam, the Iran Hostage Crisis, and the election of Ronald Reagan. As would my starting grade school, graduating from college, getting married, having and losing my one and only child; or all of my years in Oakalla. A lot could happen in twenty years. It was no wonder people wanted to relive the best of them.

I purposely ate a late lunch because I had somewhere to go afterward and didn't want to be too early. The day was unfolding uncertainly with just enough clouds around to give one pause and just enough sun to give one hope. I wanted the sun to win out because I was long tired of winter, and even a short reprieve would be welcome. Winter never bothered me as a kid because some of the best things in my life, including Christmas, sled runs, snow days and snowball fights, basketball season, and my February birthday all occurred in winter. But it bothered me now, its length more than anything bad it threw at me. March was the start of meteorological spring in some places, but not Wisconsin and all points north. Ice out sometimes didn't come until late April or May on some northern lakes. Especially during a hard winter, as this one had been. But it seemed every winter was hard anymore, no matter what the thermometer said.

Brooke Hanson was behind the counter, wearing a turquoise turtleneck sweater under her white pharmacist coat. I waited while she dispensed some pills to a customer, patiently answered all of the customer's many questions, and listened to all of the customer's many aches and pains with a sympathetic smile. I wondered how she did it day after day. Although I too was in the public eye and an easy target, I at least could lock my office door, pull down the blinds, and take my phone off the hook.

"Good afternoon, Garth," she said, her smile worn thin. "How may I help you?"

I glanced around to make sure no one was within earshot. "I have a couple questions that, unfortunately, came up. I just wanted to get your side of the story."

"About what?" Her guard was now up, as I thought it might be. This couldn't be easy for her, even if it was a happy trip down memory lane.

"Why Pug never went to college."

Her look was unforgiving. *"Larry,* Garth. He hated that name." Which was exactly what Barbara Hanson had told me. But that didn't make it so.

"Force of habit. But is that a fair question?"

"That depends on why you're asking it. If it's for the record, no. If it's to avoid a misunderstanding, yes."

"It's to avoid a misunderstanding, now and in the future. I like to know the truth, whether I do anything with it or not. It keeps me from passing judgment."

Her eyes brightened. "I would think it might have the opposite effect, depending on what the truth was."

Then a customer came into the pharmacy with a worried look on her face and came straight to the counter to stand behind me. Brooke cleared her throat ever so gently. I took that as my cue and left.

I never got back to Brooke Hanson. I had a paper to publish within thirty-six hours, and while the feature was writing itself, the rest of the paper was not. Usually it was the other way around, as I struggled to say something apt and meaningful without preaching, or climbing atop my soapbox, which was Ruth's pet peeve and for which I got low marks from her every time. Besides, I doubted Brooke Hanson would be any more forthcoming than she had been. For the hard case that Barbara Hanson appeared, I had learned more about Pug Hanson from her that I had his wife. The only question to be resolved was whether any of it was true.

It wasn't with gladness, then, when I looked up and saw George Peterson enter my office, bringing his large presence and the smell of his taxidermy shop with him. George could take up more space simply by being there than anyone I ever knew, and more oxygen. Neither did he sit in one of my hard, straight-back, Shaker chairs, chosen carefully to discourage long visits, but leaned on my desk with his thick hands spread across it and his nose inches away from my face. I leaned back to give me some breathing room and thought George was going to fall on his face, as he tried to lean with me.

"Yes, George, what is it?" I said.

"You were pretty hard on Barbara this morning. I wouldn't have thought that of you."

"She told you that?" That didn't sound like the Barbara Hanson I knew, who was fully capable of fighting her own battles.

"She didn't have to. I was there this morning, listening through the door."

"Then you need to have your hearing checked."

"My eyes, too. She was crying when she came back into the house."

"If she was, that had nothing to do with me."

"Or that letter jacket she carried? What possessed you, Garth? That's what I want to know."

Damn! I had forgotten about that. And now I had the Hulk about to take my measure. But I was proud of George for coming to her defense. I didn't know he had it in him.

"I'm sorry. I didn't mean to stir up bad memories for her," I said.

"What did you mean then, by taking that jacket?"

I could tell him the truth and have it all over town by the time I left work, or I could lie to him, or I could try to bluff him. The one thing I couldn't do was ignore him and have to work around him for the rest of the day. I didn't think we'd come to blows unless I started it, but I didn't want to put that burden on myself. I decided to try to bluff him. I produced my wallet and laid it open on the desk in front of him so that he might see my Special Deputy badge.

I said, "A long time ago the best lawman I ever knew gave that to me. It has been a burden to me ever since, and more than once I've wanted to toss it someplace dark and deep where no one could ever find it again. But as long as I'm carrying it, I'll honor it. And that's all I have to say." All true, but what I didn't tell him was that Rupert Roberts and I were three Wild Turkeys to the wind at the time.

He was a long time examining the badge. Then he straightened and handed my wallet back to me. "I thought this was all about basketball. You never said it was a police matter."

"I wear many hats, George." But that's all I said. He could draw his own conclusions.

He left without further comment. I doubted that he would say anything to anybody else now that I had flashed my badge because that would draw all the attention to him, and while George liked attention, he didn't like scrutiny. Also, I had shown Barbara that very same badge earlier in the day, so it wasn't as if I were hiding it. What puzzled me was not George's sincerity, but his intentions. Why, really, had he stepped so far out of his comfort zone to confront me, when a phone call would do. It almost seemed as if he wanted to rattle my cage. If so, it had worked.

Chapter 9

Thursday dawned a lovely day and remained so throughout. In fact, the next few days were to be unusually dry and mild for March until a cold front ended it all sometime on Monday. I ate an early supper at the Corner Bar and Grill and then went to work finishing up that week's edition of the *Reporter* before my printer arrived to put it to bed. I'd had other editions that I liked better, many of them, but none so scrutinized as this one. It was almost as if my readers couldn't wait to prove me wrong. Or somebody wrong, since there were so many opinions out there. I'd never seen the citizens of Oakalla so excited about anything else that I had done, and it made me nervous, even cautious, about every word I wrote. I didn't like the feeling. What had started out as a ruse had turned into a deal, and I had nobody to blame but myself. The worst part of it was that I had the sinking feeling that I was going to have to turn around and do it all again next week. Either that or face the wrath of my subscribers. "O what a tangled web we weave..." Shakespeare wrote. Old Bill, I had long ago come to realize, was dead on about a lot of things.

The phone rang. I hesitated to answer it because I didn't want to be bothered so close to my deadline. But then again, one never knew who might be calling. "Oakalla Reporter," I said.

"Hello, my love. How's it going?" Abby said.

"It goes. How about with you?"

"About the same. I'm on my way home, but I knew you'd be going to press later, so I didn't want to bother you then."

"About what?"

"The DNA results. We have a match."

"Crap," I said. "I was afraid of that."

"Sorry. I thought you might be happy about it. It does simplify matters."

"Agreed. But in my heart of hearts, I wanted Pug Hanson off somewhere living the life he'd always imagined."

"Do you think he was capable—of ever doing that?"

"Probably not. Definitely not, as it now appears."

"So what do we do now?"

"Await developments, if there are any. I'm hoping tomorrow's paper will shake something loose."

"And if there aren't any developments?"

"We punt, then hope for a break somewhere down the line. We've run this string about as far as we can without giving ourselves away." I lost her for a moment and realized that she was talking on her cell phone. While driving through Madison in Friday night rush hour traffic. When she came back on, I said, "You're cutting out. I'm hanging up now."

"Talk to you later then. Love you."

"Likewise, I'm sure."

After she broke the connection, I sat a while listening to my phone beep, which at that particular moment sounded strangely like a heart beat. Life was too fragile to ever be taken for granted. All it took was a cell phone call from the interstate during rush hour to tell me that.

I was back at my office by eight the next morning, awaiting the phone calls. And when they came, they came in a torrent. I'd no sooner finish one than get another. Most were complimentary. The best thing I had ever done. Blah blah, blah blah, blah blah. A few were critical without being mean spirited, pointing out things I had overlooked in an otherwise fine story. A very few were sour grapes, but I got those every week. You couldn't satisfy some people with their own, hand-written obituary. But in the midst of all the noise, I realized that I had created a controversy. Not everyone thought that this team was the best that Oakalla had ever produced. An equal number thought that honor belonged to Keith Miller's team for the simple reason that it had gone to the final game before losing. I couldn't fault that logic, which meant that the debate would play out at least another week whether I wanted it to or not. I wished that they would have been as equally divided in their opinion as to who was Oakalla's best player, but Keith Miller was nearly a unanimous choice with few detractors. It surprised me then when Tim Robinson called and begged to differ.

"Statistics don't lie, Garth. Just look at their scoring average over four years. And games won."

"I did look at their scoring average. In his best year, Pug never scored what Keith did in his worst."

"I'm not talking about Pug. I'm talking about Marcus Milner. Throw in free throws made and you have a trifecta. By your standards."

"You're playing the devil's advocate, aren't you, Tim?"

"Somebody has to, before we all go about anointing someone."

"Are you sure it's Keith Miller we're talking about?"

"Just saying, Garth." He hung up.

I wasn't expecting the next phone call. At least not so soon. "You surprised me, Garth," Barbara Hanson said. "I'll at least give you that much."

"In what way surprised you?"

"You were fair to Larry. You didn't try to make him more or less than he was. You let the facts speak for themselves. You just didn't tell the whole story."

"I couldn't because I don't know it. Just your side of it."

"I told you the truth, Garth. Make of it what you will." She hung up.

I walked to the Corner Bar and Grill for lunch, which I normally didn't do on a Friday because I knew I'd take my lumps, and after a long hard day and night at the office, I wasn't quite ready for that. But today was different. If I was to be a lightning rod, some good might come out of it.

I didn't have long to wait. I'd just sat down at the bar when Doyle Nelson took a seat beside me. "You sure have a strange choice of heroes," Doyle said.

Doyle Nelson was Emily Nelson's father, and the owner of the Pizza Place, a small dine in and carry out operation located just south of the cheese plant on Maple Street, which a block south, at the Y with Madison Road, became Railroad Street, then Fickle Road when it crossed the railroad. About my height with smooth olive skin, an oval face, dark brown, deep set eyes, and just a fringe of black hair around his otherwise bald head, Doyle had been a jack of all trades, including carnival barker, auctioneer, insurance salesman, musician, and past owner of the now defunct Dairy Barn in the east end of town. Over the years, he and I had tipped a few there at that same bar at which we were now sitting—in likely the very same seats. But I could tell by glaze over his eyes that he had a head start on me today.

"How so?" I said.

"Pug Hanson. You know that son-of-a-bitch got my daughter pregnant and then ran off with her after the baby was born." He wasn't quite slurring his words, but it still sounded like "drunk speak," when your brain shuts down and your mouth takes over, and you become wise beyond all limits of endurance.

"No. I didn't know that," I said. "How do you know that? Did she tell you?"

"She didn't have to. You can tell when something's going on. At least I can. Hiram!" He said, wildly waving his arm. "Get my friend, Garth, here a drink. And bring me another while you're at it."

"What are you having, Garth?" Hiram said.

I thought about it. I thought about a lot of things, actually, and decided I owed him this much. "A shot of Wild Turkey 101 and a draft of Leinenkugel's."

Doyle Nelson gave out a loud whistle, drawing the attention of all our bar mates. "Wild turkey! Now, there's a man for you! Not like that child stealing, snake in the grass, Pug Hanson!"

Oh shit, I thought. Here we go. I was about to be in the middle of a bar fight, and on the losing end. As the saying went, Doyle couldn't punch his way out of a wet paper bag, and I wasn't far behind him.

"Tone it down, Doyle," Hiram said. "Or I'm going to have to ask you to leave."

"You can ask," Doyle said. "But I'm not going anywhere."

The irony of such a standoff, if it came to that, was that Doyle and Hiram were good friends, and on a slow night at the Corner Bar and Grill sometimes entertained the regulars with a little picking and grinning, Hiram on harmonica and Doyle on banjo. Hiram gave me a look that said for me to do something, and then went to get our drinks.

I said, "Doyle, give me a for instance. About Pug and Emily. How do you know he got her pregnant and how do you know he was the one she ran off with? Did you see them leave together?"

"Didn't have to. I know the sound of that car as well as the sound of my own heart. It used to be mine. Until that son-of-a-bitch beat me out of it."

The car to which he was referring was Pug's maroon Dodge Charger that he had restored to new after Jimmy Collier wrecked it, and then taken ownership when Jimmy couldn't pay the bill. I didn't know until now that it had once belonged to Doyle Nelson.

Doyle was tapping his fingers on the bar, his eyes on Hiram the whole time. Once he slept this off, Doyle would be the repentant sinner—until his next bender, which could be six hours or six days or six months from now. We in Oakalla had gotten used to it because Doyle was all talk, and essentially, harmless. For the most part anyway. Unless you counted the weight of his words, which could be quite a load sometimes.

"How did he beat you out of it?" I said. "It wasn't even your car at the time."

"It should have been, though. If I hadn't gotten myself into a pinch and then had to sell it to that gear-head. Bad enough I almost had one for a son-in-law. But to have to sell my pride and joy to the likes of Jimmy Collier..." He shook his head in disbelief. "How low the mighty have fallen, Garth."

There is something incredibly sad about that which is given as fact, taken as confession. Yet, is neither.

"But to answer your question, me and Pug had a deal. He'd fix the Charger up and then sell it back to me the minute I could meet his price. Which I did. Except he wouldn't sell it back to me. He said he'd figured wrong, and I owed him more money. I showed him his original estimate. He said that didn't matter. Things had come up. He wouldn't budge. Neither would I. Then the next thing I know, he's got Emily pregnant, and then runs off with her after Billy is born." He slammed his fist down on the bar. "Bastard!"

Hiram brought us our drinks. I downed the Wild Turkey and then waited for it to kick in. What the hell. If it was going to be that kind of day, I might as well enjoy it. Meanwhile Doyle hadn't touched his Scotch and water. His anger spent, melancholy had started to set in.

"Emily had a boyfriend," I said. "Why couldn't Billy belong to him?"

"Could have, for all I know. But tell me this, Garth. Why didn't she leave with him, then?" He downed his Scotch and soda in one long swallow and said, "And she never said she hated Jared, like I overheard her tell her mother that she did

Pug. You can ask Heather, if you don't believe me." Heather was Doyle's wife.

Then Dole climbed down from his bar stool, took a moment to steady himself, and left by the north door. He might remember to pay later. He might not. Doyle was good at incurring, and forgetting, debts, which was he was better at sales than accounting.

"Thanks, Garth," Hiram said to me after Doyle left. "He can be a handful when he gets like that."

"I wonder what set him off?"

"Your paper, I reckon. He came in here carrying it and was reading it up until the time he wadded it up and threw it on the floor. You want an extra copy, I can go get it for you. The way they're going, you might need it."

"After all these years," I said. "And I wasn't even trying."

"What's that, Garth?"

"Nothing, Hiram. Did you overhear any of what Doyle said?"

"Darn near all of it, as I imagine everybody else in here did too."

"What do you think about his car story? Does any of it hold water?"

"The part about once owning it does. He loved that car. It broke his heart when he had to sell it. As for the rest of it, you might ask Danny Palmer. He and Pug were good friends, and they practically worked side by side together for several years."

Which I knew all too well and was why I hesitated to involve Danny any further than he was. It wasn't easy to be objective about your friends, especially those with whom you've worked hand in hand at hard labor.

"What's your take on Pug?" I said. "Do you think he could have done what Doyle says he did?"

"Garth, you're talking to a man who's been a bartender going on forty years now. What I haven't heard isn't worth telling, the good and the bad. But Pug wasn't in here much. Like Danny, he'd just stop by for beer every now and again, especially on a hot summer day. But just one, and that was it. Like he once said to me, he'd give five dollars for that first beer, but not five cents for the second. I wish some others around here would take that to heart."

"Don't wish away your regulars, Hiram. They're what keep you in business."

"I'd rather lose the business than them their hard earned pay. But that's up to them, I guess."

He went back to tending bar. I drank the rest of my Leinenkugel's, paid for my drinks, and left.

Danny Palmer was nowhere to be found. Sniffy said he'd gone to start someone's car and would be back shortly. Did I want any peanuts while I waited? I said yes. They tasted good on any empty stomach and helped quiet the buzz in my brain.

"You okay, Garth?" Sniffy asked with concern.

"I will be. Just remind me not to do that again on an empty stomach."

"Do what?"

"Honor the dead."

"You're not making any sense, you know that."

"'Much madness is divinest sense,' Sniffy. You'd do well to remember that."

"Have you been drinking? That's not like you. At least not in the middle of the day. But I guess a little celebration is in order. You knocked the lights out this week, Garth. I've not seen the people around here as excited about anything in a coon's age."

"As they say, timing is everything. Do the same story in July, and see what I'd get. But what do you think, Sniffy? Which team was best?"

Sniffy puffed up, as he was wont to do whenever his opinion carried weight, and gave out with a couple loud sniffs. "Keith Miller's was a one man team. Anyone with eyes could see that. Stop him and you could stop them."

"Except nobody did stop him. At least not his senior year."

"Not until they met a better team. Ten points is all he got in that game. He was averaging twenty-five."

"Twenty-seven, according to Tim Robinson. But who's counting?"

"It looks like you and Tim are. The little prick. Thinks he know everything about everything. My point is, Garth, you had to stop two people on Pug Hanson's team, him and Wonder Boy. Both of them could score at will. Pug just chose not to because he wanted to get all of his teammates involved. He scored forty-five points in one game, a record that still stands. All because Wonder Boy sat on the bench with four fouls most of the last three quarters, before finally fouling out. All he ever had to learn to do was move his feet on defense, which he never did. And move without the ball. And he'd been right up there with Pug and Keith. As for who was best between them, there's not an eyelash worth of difference. But my vote goes to Pug because he could score from anywhere on the court. Keith got most of his baskets in the paint. What do you think, Danny?"

I was surprised to look around and see Danny Palmer standing behind me. And relieved. Once Sniffy got on a roll, there was usually no stopping him.

"I think there's a customer in the drive, Sniffy. If you don't mind, since she came on your watch."

"Who is it?"

"Sheila Rodgers."

Sniffy was off his stool and out the door like a shot.

"Who's Sheila Rodgers?" I asked.

"New girl in town. Well, young woman. I think Sniffy's sweet on her. What can I do for you, Garth, so early in the day?"

It was a running joke between us. Early could be any time before six, his usual quitting time. We did a lot of our business after hours.

"I was just talking to Doyle Nelson up at the Corner. He said he has proof that Emily ran off with Pug."

"What's his proof?"

"Pug's Dodge Charger. He said he heard it outside his door the night Emily disappeared. He also said Pug beat him out of it by changing his estimate after the fact."

"That was because Jimmy Collier ran the crap out of it before he wrecked it, and Pug and I had to completely rebuild the engine. That was my bill Pug added on. Not his. I said for the sake of peace for Pug to forget it, but he said no way, that Doyle knew going in the estimate might change, depending on what we found. That's why they call it an estimate. Pug liked that car, but he wasn't in love with it, as Doyle was. He only intended to keep it until Doyle paid me for my work. But Doyle never did, so Pug paid me the difference, and kept it for himself. You have long enough, I can probably show you the invoice. I don't throw anything like that away because of taxes."

"No, I'll take your word for it."

Then Danny shook his his head, angry at himself. "Darn it, Garth, I had something else I wanted to tell you, something important. But it's gone now. Never mind. I might think of it later."

"Then it could have been Pug after all?"

"I guess. Anything's possible. And Pug did tell me not long before he left that he wasn't happy with his marriage, which I'd sort of known for a long time, although he didn't come right out and say it. But him fooling around with a sixteen-year-old girl? I don't buy that, Garth. That wasn't Pug."

"What was Pug?"

"A straight shooter. As straight as they come."

"What about his wife? Was she a straight shooter?"

"No comment, Garth. Pug never said one way or another. Other people have, though. She got around more than you might think."

"Before or after they were married?"

"Before, I think. I hear she pretty much settled down afterward. But you didn't hear any of this from me."

Wearing a large smile, Sniffy was on his way in from the drive. "Thanks, Danny. If you think of anything else, let me know."

"That I'll do. And, Garth, just between you and me, were those Pug's bones you found?"

"Yes. Just between you and me."

"For sure?" He didn't want to believe it.

"For sure. Abby had someone run his DNA."

"Then that lets him off the hook, doesn't it? He couldn't have run off with Emily Nelson, not if he was dead."

"Emily Nelson didn't leave town until a year after Pug did. We don't know where he was in the meantime, or that he didn't come back after her."

"Not likely, though."

Still all smiles, Sniffy's feet barely touched the ground as he came into the building. "No. Not likely," I said.

"What isn't likely?" Sniffy said. "And why the long faces?"

"That I'll ever live in the country," I said.

"Why?" Sniffy said, suddenly on the alert. "You're not thinking of moving, are you?"

"It's a long story, Sniffy. One not likely to have a happy ending." I left in the direction of home.

Chapter 10

I met Ruth at the Corner Bar and Grill on her way home from the shelter. Since it was all you can eat fish night, I wanted to get there early so we would have a place to to sit. Abby was working the emergency room at the hospital. Liddy Bennett was covering for Ruth at the shelter. We could eat at our leisure and then leave before it got wall to wall in there. Or so I thought. We took the last available booth in the dining room. There was more room in the bar, but Ruth had never liked to sit in there because of all the drunks about. So she said anyway. I thought it had more to do with the way she was raised, in that a lady avoided the barroom if possible, and never ever sat at the bar. Abby, however, preferred the barroom. In the past because she could smoke in there. In the present, now that she no longer smoked, because she liked its people better than those in the dining room. Drinkers and smokers, even reformed ones, just naturally got along, she said. Who was I to argue?

"What's the rush?" Ruth said.

"It's yellow perch night." Except for walleye, we both liked yellow perch better than anything else. Between them, it was a toss-up.

"Good," she said. "I thought it might have been something else."

"For instance?"

"A pat on the back for that article of yours."

"From you? I know better."

"No. From every Tom, Dick, and Harry that walks in here tonight."

"They'll be too busy talking basketball in real time. Besides, not everybody wants to give me a pat on the back. I found that out at noon, when Doyle Nelson climbed all over me."

Pat Winters came to take our order. She was a perfect Friday night waitress. Right to the point and fast on her feet. We ordered fish and a pitcher of Leinenkugel's. When the pitcher was empty, we'd leave.

"What put the bee in his bonnet this time?" Ruth said.

"Pug Hanson. He called him a child thief, or something to that effect."

"A child stealer," Herb Cooper said from right beside me on his way into the bar.

"I stand corrected. A child stealer."

"He's got a lot of room to talk," Ruth said.

"Tell me more."

"You know I don't like the man, Garth. Why stir up trouble?"

Ruth and Doyle's feud went a long way back to the time he hit on her shortly after Ruth's husband, Karl, died. The fact that she was two decades older than he didn't seem to bother Doyle, but it did Ruth. She once said that he would chase any skirt as long as it was still moving.

"Humor me," I said.

Pat brought us our pitcher of beer. I poured us each a glass and took a deep drink of mine. It had been a sleepy afternoon, especially after my noon salvo wore off. I needed something to jump start me again before I dozed off.

"You get any sleep at all last night?" Ruth said.

"Not much. I was too hyped."

"That's what I figured. You always drink to stay awake."

I had to smile. She knew me well. Then I raised my glass and touched it to hers.

"What's that for?" she said.

"The good times."

She gave me a rare smile. "There have been a few, haven't there."

"That there have."

"But this isn't one of them. I don't like talking about Doyle Nelson. It's not my place."

"Not even to help me?"

"Do what? Ruin somebody else's life. You do a good enough job of that on your own."

"I don't ruin anybody's life, Ruth. In Doyle's case, he doesn't need any help with that. I just sort out the broken pieces, to see how they fit."

She gave it some thought, then said, "Just a rumor, that's all, back when he was running the Dairy Barn. A lot of high school girls worked there then. It was said he took a shine to one of them and she to him."

"And her name?"

But all Ruth said was, "Talk about the devil."

I turned around as discreetly as possible to look behind me. Marcus Milner and Brooke Hanson stood just a few feet away, searching in vain for an empty booth, or at worst, two empty stools at the counter. There weren't any. Then they came to stand beside me.

"Do you mind, Garth?" Marcus said.

"No, I don't mind. How about you, Ruth?"

She minded, which was why she didn't say anything.

"It's just until something opens up," Marcus said. "I've already put our name in."

Ruth scooted over. I followed suit. Marcus sat beside Ruth, Brooke beside me. He gave Ruth a wide berth between them. Brooke sat close enough for our legs to touch every time one of us moved. I couldn't help but notice her perfume. It smelled like lilac. She must have showered after work. Her hair was still wet.

"So where's Howard?" I said. Howdy Hanson was often with them on a Friday night, usually in the company of Billy Nelson.

"Over at the Pizza Place," Brooke said. "Howard's spending the night with Billy. But it's yet to be determined at whose house."

Doyle and Heather Nelson and Marcus Milner and Brooke Hanson were neighbors of sorts. They lived on the west side of Home Street a block apart in the second block north of me, the Nelson's on the far south end of the block, and Marcus and Brooke on the far north end, which was also at the end of the street. It was all pasture, wood, and field beyond them.

"Sounds like a plan," I said, remembering with a smile my own sleepovers.

"They think so anyway," Marcus said. Then he went on to say, "Good article today, Garth. I think you were fair to all concerned, especially me. You could have done a hatchet job on me. But you didn't."

Neither Marcus nor Brooke had dressed down after work. Marcus wore a navy sport coat over a sky blue shirt open at the collar and Brooke a black sweater over a white blouse buttoned at the top. Both did wear jeans, however, if one called that dressing down.

"I tried to let the facts speak for themselves. You had a great season. There was no way around that."

"Me or the team?"

"All of you."

"Except the ending."

"Stuff happens, Marcus. With the best of intentions, we can dig our own grave."

He seemed to take it all in stride. Brooke, however, said, "That's a strange choice of words, Garth. It's not like Marcus lost the ball on purpose."

"What he is saying, my love, is that we can try to do the right thing, but it turns out to be the wrong thing. That's all."

"I know what he's saying, Marcus. I just didn't like his choice of words. It was just a ballgame after all, not a Pork Chop Hill. Let's not all lose our perspective here."

"I agree," Ruth said. "Or our appetites."

I was thankful that Pat chose that moment to tell them that a table in the bar had opened up, if they wanted it. Brooke said that they did. Then she said to me, "So this is the end of it, I hope. I thought I'd enjoy the trip down memory lane. But I didn't."

"I wish, but I can't promise you anything," I said. "There seems to be a difference of opinion as far as which team was the all-time best. That debate still needs to play out. But after next week, it's done. No matter what."

"Well, you can count me out now," she said. "I'm done. No matter what."

"You can count me in," Marcus said, as he slid out of the booth and offered his hand. "I'm enjoying my day in the sun."

I shook his hand, which swallowed mine in a warm embrace. "I wish I could say the same, Marcus."

Ruth waited until they were well inside the bar before saying, "It sure didn't take much effort on your part to cozy up to her. You're lucky Abby didn't walk in about then."

"What did you expect me to do, Ruth, sit in the window? I gave her as much room as I could."

"Tell me another one. You liked having her there, and you know it."

Guilty as charged, but it had nothing to do with anything. The day that I didn't enjoy the near presence of a pretty woman was the day they hung a wreath on my door. But I didn't expect Ruth to understand. Despite her aversion to the "good old days," she was, in many ways, much more old school than I.

"You never finished telling me what you said you were going to," I said.

"Yes, I did. You just weren't listening."

"Are you saying that Brooke Hanson and Doyle Nelson had something going while she was still in high school?"

"It was Brooke Childers then, but yes, that's what I'm saying. It cost her, her job, and him his first marriage when his wife found out about it."

"Heather isn't his first wife?"

"No. She got him on the rebound. Lucky her."

"Then she can't be Emily's mother." Which was how Doyle referred to her. I kept trying to make the numbers add up, but couldn't.

"Yes and no, Garth. You don't have to be blood to be a mother. From everything I know about her, she welcomed the job. And raising her grandson as well, which can't be easy in this age."

"Whatever happened to Doyle's first wife?"

"I don't know. She just left town one day and never came back."

"And hasn't been seen since?"

"I didn't say that. The last time I heard, she had remarried and was living in Duluth."

"From paradise to hell. She must be paying penitence for something."

"To my mind, it's the other way around. Living with Doyle Nelson is hell enough for anybody."

"Come on, Ruth. He made a pass at you. You're a beautiful woman... at any age."

"Even if that were true, that still doesn't let him off the hook. I'm old enough to be his mother. What did he think we would ever have in common?"

"Besides the obvious?"

"Don't go there, Garth. That still makes my skin crawl."

"You're old enough to be my mother. And we have a lot in common."

"Except for your taste in women."

"You like Abby."

"She's the first one. And I'll continue to like her as long as she does right by you. Now, let's eat."

I leaned back as Pat set a steaming platter of perch in front of us. "Good idea."

I stopped by the Marathon early the next morning on my way to the farm. Tired as I was when I went to bed, I had thought I would sleep in for once, but it wasn't to be. I was still too wired from that week's events. I couldn't get my mind to shut down no matter how hard I tried. I had started the week with only one thing in mind, and that was to figure out our living arrangement once Abby and I were married in July. Now, I had Pug Hanson's bones and a brewing controversy over Oakalla's best basketball team to worry about. One I could handle with ease. It would go away on its own after a while. Sooner rather than later. The other would also resolve itself—for good or for ill. But Pug's bones also demanded immediate answers, and at the moment I had none. And would have none, unless something broke in my favor.

Danny was alone in his office, sitting at his desk, while staring at the blank screen on his computer. After a late night of euchre with the guys at the Corner Bar and Grill, Sniffy wouldn't be in until late morning, if then. It all depended how his night went, and how much money he was in the hole. Sniffy didn't mind paying his debts. But he hated the ribbing that came with it.

"Morning, Garth," Danny said without looking up from his computer. "Have a seat." Then he wheeled his chair around to face me. "As you can see, I'm not busy."

Or flush with sleep. His eyes were as red as mine. "I can't stay, Danny. I'm on my way to the farm. I just stopped by to see if you had remembered anything else about Pug that I should know."

"No, I'm sorry to say. The more I rack my brain, the more frustrated I get. I hardly slept at all last night. Finally I moved to the couch so Sharon could get some sleep."

"I know the feeling. But I do have a couple questions, if you don't mind answering them."

"Fire away. For the good it'll do."

"You never know. It might do a lot of good."

"But not bring Pug back."

"No," I agreed. "Nothing will bring Pug back. But it might bring him some justice."

"That's mighty thin soup, Garth, to feed to a hungry man."

I didn't have any answers for him. I never did at times like these, which was why Ruth and I were always butting heads. Justice existed for its own sake, I had come to believe. Not to make it all better. Not to soothe anyone's soul. "It's all I have, Danny."

"What are your questions, then? Before somebody pulls in."

"This is in confidence, you understand," I said.

"What isn't lately where we're concerned? I swear, Garth. I start to sweat every time you walk in that door."

"Be that as it may, did you ever think of Pug as a suicide?"

"No. Why do you ask?"

"Because Abby thinks he might have been. At least that's her professional judgment."

"On what grounds?"

"The large hole in the back of his head that appears to be self-inflicted."

"I don't remember seeing any hole."

"Neither did I at first. Somebody had carefully covered it with plastic, and then painted it to match his skull."

"Then there you go, Garth. That proves he didn't kill himself. He couldn't very well hide his own wound after he was dead."

"Not necessarily, Danny. I mean about committing suicide."

"What are you saying, then? You just lost me."

"A thought I've been chewing on. But I don't want to say anything else until I'm sure."

"Well, when you are sure, let me know. In the meantime, we'll just leave it where it is, if you don't mind."

"I don't mind." I started to leave.

"You said you had a couple questions, Garth. You still have one left."

"I know, but it can wait. It doesn't seem all that important now."

"Ask it anyway. Before you forget."

"You still call him Pug. I was curious about what Larry really thought about that name."

"I asked him that once, because I'd heard a couple different stories on the subject. He said he hated it at first, got used to it over time, and finally learned to like it, when he realized it was meant as a compliment, not a put down. Though he did say, given his druthers, he would have rather have been called Spike. You know, after the bulldog."

"That would have been my choice, too," I said.

The drive out to the farm was a peaceful one. It was still too cool to roll the windows down, but had I been able to do so, I was sure that I would have been able to hear a cardinal singing his heart out from somewhere high in a treetop. I had once, on a simply dazzling February day, no brighter, yet much colder than this one, and it had left quite an impression because I was right in the middle of a mid-life crisis. It gave me hope where before there was none, and helped steady my ship. When I thought of the years in between then and now, it was easy to lose sight of the man I was then, easy to find fault and pass judgment, to wonder how his life could have fallen into such disrepair. But hindsight is like that.

I thought I was alone on Fair Haven Road, until I approached the turn onto Navoe Road that would take me to the farm. And eventually Navoe Cemetery, if I wanted to go that far. Then I saw a vehicle in the distance behind me. But when I pulled into Fair Haven Cemetery, and stopped, I didn't see it go on by. Curious about its whereabouts, and its occupants, I tried to wait it out, but after several minutes, gave up and drove on to the farm. If all went well there, I would stop at the cemetery again on my way back home. If it didn't all go well, there was always next time.

My first stop was at the root cellar, but there was nothing new to learn there, so I went on to the house. Once inside, I heard a vehicle approach from the east, the way I'd come, slow, but not stop. But by the time I could get to a window, it was long gone. After a few minutes in the house, I decided there was nothing new to learn there either. I still didn't want to live in the country. Nothing had occurred within the past week to change my mind about that.

I went to the barn, which still smelled like hay because the renter stored his square bales of alfalfa there, to be later sold or fed to his cattle. I stood a while, drinking it all in— the cats, the cows, the forts, the fights with my cousins, as the hay bales started to roll—the dusty, musty winter afternoons alone with my B-B gun. But there are only so many memories allowed, even good ones, before they start to overwhelm you.

I walked on down to the pond where Grandmother and I used to fish for sunfish and bluegill and where I still kept a small rowboat and oars. I flipped the boat over, put the oars in the locks, pushed off, and began to row. It was cool there in the shade along the edge of the pond, made cooler by the skim of ice melt atop the water, but when I reached the middle of the pond, and sunshine, I could feel me start to thaw. No breeze blew. Not even a ripple upon the water. Or the sight of any other living thing. Even the resident coot was nowhere to be seen.

I heard the rifle shot just after the first slug hit the water beside me. There was the slightest pause, and then another slug hit the water with a whoosh. This one was closer that the first. He was starting to get the range. I had three choices. I could either sit there like a wooden duck, or I could dive into the water and swim to the nearest shore, or I could row like hell for the far shore and hope he didn't zero in on me. The problem with the first choice became obvious when the third shot nicked my ear. The problem with the second choice was that if I didn't die from gunfire, I likely would from hypothermia (if I didn't drown first), and he would have committed the perfect crime. No car to move, no body to hide, nothing to indicate that I did done anything besides the obvious, which was to lose my balance and fall into the lake. The problem with the third choice was that, once I reached shore, what would I do then? And I would be in the open the whole way there, and beyond.

I spun the boat around and began rowing as fast as I could toward him and his position, which appeared to be a wooded knob west of the pond about three hundred yards away. If he held his ground, it was a suicide mission because I was armed only with a jackknife, and a dull one at that. But he didn't know that. My real concern, as I saw it, was that I might be shot in the meantime.

The fifth shot hit the water behind me, where I'd been the second before. It's harder to hit a target moving toward you than away from you, or so it seemed from my limited experience at duck hunting. That was my hope anyway, that and the state of his nerves, as he saw his quarry go from hunted to hunter. Most killers, except the pros, are basically cowards, who prey on the weak and vulnerable when the odds are decidedly in their favor. A fair fight is not part of their repertoire and to be avoided at all costs—which is why so many of them commit suicide once they are cornered.

I rowed all the way to shore and hit the ground running before the boat even stopped. That was adrenalin talking, which is almost as good as Wild Turkey at getting you somewhere you ought not go. I heard a sixth shot, but it was far over my head and hit the water behind me. There wasn't a seventh shot, which was good because I was running out of options. And wind, and adrenalin. To think, I used to do this for fun. Run, that is. Not face enemy fire.

I slowed my pace to a walk as I scoured the terrain ahead. It would be the cruelest of fates for him to be waiting for me at the edge of the woods. Sorry, Garth, but the joke's on you. I'm a pro, hired by your friendly neighborhood improvement authority. Except, I had known such a person, two of them in fact, and neither of them would have missed even once at three hundred yards.

There was a large dead walnut tree, top branches broken, bark peeling off its trunk, atop the knob at the edge of the woods. Around it, I found the brass of three .222 Magnum shells. The .222 is basically a target and varmint rifle that you carry around in the trunk of your car or on the rack of your pickup in case you see a feral cat or a coyote, or a Bud Light beer can, or anything else you think needs shooting. It's not a hunting rifle, especially in Wisconsin, where whitetail deer is the animal of choice; or an assassin's rifle. But it can still kill you in a heartbeat.

I had some time to think on my way back up the lane. "Know your enemy" is one of the first cardinal rules of successful warfare, right along with "know yourself." Had my enemy followed me to the farm with the singular intention of killing me? I didn't think so. Otherwise, he would have done a better job of it. He could have shot me in the barn or anywhere between there and the house, buried me under the hay, and driven Jessie as far as he could before she broke down, and no one would have been the wiser. What seemed more likely is that he had seen his chance while I was walking to the pond, and taken it. The road to Mitchell's Woods went right beside my woods, so it would be easy to park along it, grab his rifle, slip through the woods, and see what opportunity presented itself. If that proved to be nothing, he could leave as quietly as he came, and no one would be the wiser. My question was why had he followed me in the first place, if not to do me harm? The answer seemed that he feared that I might do him harm, so either my cover story hadn't worked, or I hadn't been as clever as I thought in my investigation so far. Or he was far more clever than I gave him credit for. Or far more guilty.

On reaching Jessie, I sat for a minute, soaking up the warmth and the peace. It's easy to take life for granted, even when you know better, easy to get caught in all the minutiae and the flotsam and the pride and the glory, and even the pain, large or small as it may be. Easy to assume that all this will always be there, since it's me after all. Until it's not.

Jessie started on the first try, as she had lately on every try. I took that as an ominous sign because she could never go too long before reverting to her own worse self—sort of like the girl with the curl, only worse. That meant that something big and bad was looming. But little did I realize...

Chapter 11

The phone rang the next morning just as I was about to put the water in the coffee maker. I had managed to eat a bowl of Honey Nut Cheerios and drink a glass of orange juice, but that was all I'd accomplished. I groaned aloud at the the thought of answering. It was never good news when it came this early. Especially on a Sunday.

"This is Garth," I said.

"Garth, this is Danny. You better get up here right away."

Danny Palmer was one of the few people that I knew who rarely got excited about anything. That was why he made such a good fire chief and civic leader. He could keep his cool while under fire or while fighting one. To say that I needed to get there right away likely meant the sky was falling.

"Let me get some clothes on."

"Who was that?" Ruth said on her way into the kitchen.

"Danny Palmer."

"What did he want?"

"He didn't say."

She stifled a yawn. "Then it can't be good news."

There was a warm breeze in my face all the way up Fair Haven Road to the Marathon. It felt good to be out and about, even though I was still dead on my feet and more than sore from yesterday's charge up the knoll. My ear had finally scabbed over and stopped bleeding sometime in the night, although my pillow was now a bloody mess. I told Ruth that I had scraped my ear on a low hanging limb on my way to the barn. She didn't believe me, but neither did she press the issue. There was nothing more that I could tell her anyway. Except that someone had tried to kill me.

Danny sat in his office chair. All the lights inside the station were off. He never worked on a Sunday, but there was no sense advertising the fact that he was there, or someone would invariably stop by for gas. Or for help, or to gossip. Whether Danny knew it or not, and I thought he did, along with the Corner Bar and Grill, the Marathon was the nerve center of the town, where old men and boys could go to loaf at their leisure, and one of the few places in town where men, old and young alike, could interact without rancor. I hated the thought of Danny ever closing up shop. Oakalla would be far the poorer for it.

"Have a seat, Garth," Danny said, after rising to lock the door behind me. "You'll need it."

"That bad, huh."

"Worse."

I took the nearest chair. He sat down facing me. "What did you do to your ear?" he said.

"Caught it on a low hanging tree branch out at the farm."

"I bet."

"You were never a cynic before."

"At least not before I met you," he said.

"You're not the first to tell me that."

"Misery loves company."

"Speaking of which, what do you have for me?"

He took a deep breath, and slowly exhaled. "You remember you asked me yesterday afternoon if I thought Pug might be a suicide, and I said no. Well, it got me to thinking, and thinking, and thinking. I thought about it all last evening and was still thinking about it when I finally drifted off to sleep somewhere around midnight. This morning I remembered. The week before Pug disappeared, I happened to walk over to his shop to talk to him about something, or borrow something, since we were always lending tools back and forth. What I didn't have, he did. Or vice versa. Anyway, when I walked into his shop, the first thing I noticed was how clean it was. Not that Pug kept a messy shop. A place for everything, and everything in its place, that was Pug. But there weren't any cars in there to be fixed. Not even a go-cart. I asked Pug what the deal was because normally the place was full of wrecked cars, and he gave me a funny look, and said he was clearing the decks in case something happened. Those were his exact words, Garth, 'in case something happened.' I asked him what was he talking about, was he sick or something? But he never would answer, which wasn't like him because we didn't keep any secrets between us. Or at least I didn't think so at the time."

Danny got up to pour himself a cup of coffee. I followed suit. It was going to be a long miserable day for all concerned without one.

Danny said, "So then I thought maybe I was wrong. Maybe he did kill himself. Then I remembered something else that threw that notion clear out of whack. Pug had been having trouble with his car. He thought it might be the fuel pump, but he wasn't sure, so he wanted me to take a look at it. I think I might have even have scheduled it, but I can't find the paperwork, even if there was any, that being so long ago. But I know it happened. Which makes no sense when you think about it. Why would he leave town in a car that he knew might quit on him a mile down the road?"

"Are you saying that the car never left town, Danny?"

"No. It never left town. It's still here. In his shop. Right next door."

"What made you think to look there?"

"A couple things, Garth. One, that shop's not had any traffic for ten years. It's in Pug's name, so nobody else could do anything with it as long as he was alive. Except pay taxes, which I assume Brooke did. Or somebody did anyway, or the county would own it by now. So if it didn't have any traffic, and it was clean the last time I was in there, why was there something covered up in there? I mean I walk right by it every day on my way to work. It's kind of hard not to peek inside every now and again, just to see how things are holding up."

"And the second thing?"

"Years ago, and I mean years ago, I kept smelling something dead. I thought maybe a rat, or some other rodent, had crawled in here and died. But I never could find it, and eventually the smell went away. That did get me to thinking, though, when I started putting two and two together this morning, about that thing under wraps there in Pug's shop."

"Do I want to see for myself?" I said.

"No, Garth. You don't."

Danny and I carefully removed the canvas drop cloth from Pug's Dodge Charger, carefully folded it, and set it atop the pile of other carefully folded drop cloths. Although we both knew Pug was dead, we wanted to leave the shop as he had left it and not violate the order of the place.

Considering its age and history, the Charger was in remarkable condition. There were some mud splatters along both sides, and on the hubcaps and bumpers, but its chrome still shown and its paint looked new. Even on the inside, except for some gravel here and there on the floor mats, Pug's careful detailing was still evident, as well preserved as if the car had been in a museum. The keys were still in the ignition. It almost seemed a shame to open the trunk.

I didn't find there what I thought I would, which were the remnants of Pug's clothes. Instead, I found the still clothed skeleton of what appeared to be a young woman curled around a travel bag. Even after all the years, the smell of death was still strong. Five would get me ten that this body had never been moved.

"Have you looked inside the travel bag?" I said.

"No. Here is as far as I got."

"Then maybe we should."

The travel bag was red-and-white with a cartoon Bucky Badger on it. Bucky was smiling. I guess he couldn't help himself, but under the circumstances, it seemed out of place. A mouse had eaten a hole in one corner of the bag and left a nest inside, but the rest seemed to be intact. I hated to dig around in there because it seemed a violation of sorts. And there was also the outside chance that the mouse might take exception. But I needed identification, if there was any. It turned out there was. The bag belonged to Emily Nelson.

I put the wallet back inside the bag, the bag back inside the trunk, and closed the lid. Then Danny and I re-covered the car with the drop cloth and locked the back door of the shop on our way out.

"What did she look like in life?" I said once we were back inside the Marathon. "I forget."

"Who?"

"Emily Nelson."

"A whole lot like Brooke Hanson did at that age. Why?"

"I just wondered," I said.

"Are you telling Abby about this?"

"No. We're not telling anybody."

"We can't sit on this forever, Garth. It's not right in a whole lot of ways."

"I don't plan to. But she's been hidden there for years now. A few more days won't hurt. There is one thing, Danny, to cover your butt in case it comes to that. If Pug's shop was locked, how did you get in there in the first place?"

"I have a key, just as Pug had a key to my place. As I said, we never knew when we might need to borrow something from each other, and with the hours we both kept, especially Pug, we just thought it was the smart thing to do."

"And Pug never told you why he was unhappy in his marriage?"

"No. He never said."

I excused myself and went into Danny's bathroom to wash my hands, which smelled like mouse urine. When I came back out, Danny was already at the door.

"We're done here, aren't we?" he said.

"Yes. For now."

"Well, at least we know one thing."

"What's that, Danny?"

"She didn't commit suicide. Pug either, I'm thinking."

"You're right about her. You might be right about Pug. I'm reserving judgment for now."

"Do you think he came back to kill her, and then killed himself? That's crazy, Garth, and we both know it. He couldn't even have left town. Not with a bad fuel pump."

"Indulge me a moment, Danny. We don't know he had a bad fuel pump. He only told you he had a bad fuel pump."

"Okay, Garth, even if I give you that, which I don't because it wasn't like Pug to lie, why would he wait a year before coming back and killing her? That makes no sense at all."

"Maybe she wanted to wait until after she had her child. Maybe he couldn't stand the pressure in the meantime. Maybe he didn't intend to kill her, but it just happened. It does sometimes when we're under stress. I'm just throwing things out there, trying to see what sticks. No, I don't think Pug killed her, or that he ever left town, but there's a big black hole that I can't penetrate, and until I do, I'm not closing any doors."

"That's why you're better at this than I am. I would have closed those doors long ago."

As if to prove his point, he closed the door on me. I had to let myself out.

The warm south wind pushed me all the way home. I gave us until tomorrow before reality set in and winter returned with a vengeance. The only good thing about it was that its return would be short lived. In fits and starts, that's how spring came in Wisconsin. More fits than starts, but before I knew it, summer would be here and gone, and the geese flying south again. Or the Sandhill Cranes that I always mistook for geese. I always welcomed their return. I always hated to see them go. Expectations are better than memories because they require so little revision.

Jared Cox lived on the last farm along Fair Haven Road before you got to the church and cemetery. It wasn't a farm as such, but, like mine, the shell of one. Its Holsteins, Berkshires, and Road Island Reds were all gone, along with its wheat, oats, and pastures, most of its fence rows, and all of its hues. Its outbuildings were still used to store tools and equipment, and its barn to store hay, but its fields grew only corn and soybeans, and its owners, Jared's parents, now lived in town. I didn't blame them. It was easier to rent than to farm, and the money a whole lot more certain.

Jared had vehicles in various states of repair all over the place, so it was hard to know which were his and which belonged to friends of his. As a shade tree mechanic, rough carpenter, and heralded local race car driver, he would try to fix anything he got his hands on, if not to make it better, at least faster. But when he reached that point beyond his knowledge, without fail, he always went to Danny for advice, which Danny happily gave him. Danny said that if he ever decided to hire someone to help him, it would be Jared. And if not for all the rules and regulations that came with it, he would have already have hired him because he thought so much of Jared's work. In the land of wrench and ratchet, that was high praise. High praise indeed.

I found Jared Cox outside working on a car—a stock car by the looks of it with mud caked all the way to its roof and the number seven painted on both sides. "Morning, Garth," Jared said, stopping to shake my hand. "What are you doing out this way again so soon?"

"So soon?"

"Yeah, I saw you drive by in that car of yours yesterday morning. It's hard to miss, if you know what I mean."

"What direction was I going?"

"South. Toward Oakalla."

"You didn't see me on my way out to the farm?" If so, he might have seen the person following me.

"No. I wasn't up that early. Late night with friends," he said as a way of explanation. "Give me a minute and I'll be right with you."

"Take all the time you need."

"Don't tell me that, Garth, or you'll be here all day. I've got to get this baby running right before the season starts. My test run didn't go so well yesterday."

So I watched him as he worked, fascinated not only with his dedication, but that anyone could get so much pleasure out of a car. Even a race car. I could see the driving part, and the thrill a minute that went with it, but not all the rest, especially the work and the expense. Said he, who was still driving Jessie after all these years. But I never pretended to love, even like her.

Then I took a moment to study Jared himself and see if I could find the likeness between him and Billy Nelson. I couldn't. Billy was slender to the point of skinny with large brown eyes, short brown hair, and a dark olive complexion like that of his grandfather, Doyle. In fact, he looked a lot like his grandfather, so much so that they could pass for father and son. Jared, on the other hand, was large framed and big boned with a ruddy complexion, small blue-black eyes, and long, unruly, blond hair that complemented the tattoos of an America flag on his left arm and a white number three in a black oval on the right. Try though I might, I couldn't put them in the same family, let alone as father and son.

Jared finished his adjustments, wiped his hand on a rag, and went over to his cooler and pulled out two Silver Bullets, offering one of them to me. Hating to appear rude, I took it. Besides, it was warm there in the sun.

"Why don't you work on this inside?" I said.

"Because inside is all full. So what's on your mind, Garth?" he said, suddenly all business. "I know this isn't about basketball."

"It is, and it isn't. Apparently you also know I did a feature on Pug Hanson and his teammates last week. This is just a follow up."

"And you want to know who Billy Nelson's real father is. So do I, Garth. But I can't tell you."

"Then he could be yours?"

"He should be mine. I just don't think he is. Pug's either for that matter."

"Why do you say that?"

"That wasn't Pug's style. At least what I knew of the man. Early on, he was as quick to help me as Danny was. At least until the rumors started. Then we both started backing off. You have to remember, I'm a few years older than Emily. If she was pregnant, my tit was also in the ringer."

"How many is a few?"

"Four. I guess she just liked older men."

"Did she ever say anything about Pug, like, for example, that she hated him?"

"Who told you that?"

"Doyle Nelson."

"Now, there's a piece of work, Garth. If Emily ever hated anyone, it was him."

"Did she say why?"

But he had already moved on to another thought. "Now that you mention it, there was a guy she said she did hate. We were standing in the gym at the time. She had just finished showering after practice, when she came right out and said it.'I hate him. He gives me the creeps.' When I asked if it was Pug, she said, him too, but no, it was the guy standing there with him. She said he was always trying to sneak a peek at her when she was undressing. She wouldn't be surprised if he didn't have a hidden camera there in the girls' locker room."

"Who was the guy standing there with Pug?"

"I don't remember his name. The janitor. That's all I know."

"Tim Robinson?"

"That sounds like it. Sort of a sour looking guy that always keeps to himself?"

"Yes. That would be Tim."

"One last question, Jared. Have you heard anything from Emily since she left town?" Although I already knew the answer, I wanted to see his reaction.

"No. Not that first word. But it's not all that surprising. Long before the baby was ever born, we had started to drift apart to the point where we had stopped seeing each other. I told her that if the baby was mine, I'd be glad to pay support, but she said no, it would be better if I would just get out of her life and stay there. Which I did."

"Do you know why you drifted apart?"

"If I was that smart, Garth, to be able to read a woman's mind, I wouldn't be framing houses for a living."

"Are you saying it was all on her part?"

"Pretty much. I even offered to marry her as soon as I knew for sure she was pregnant, but she said no, she wasn't ready for that yet. When I asked her when she would be ready, she never would give me an answer. That's when I began to see the writing on the wall."

"Do you think she was involved with someone else? I mean, not counting you or Pug."

"I've often wondered. If so, he was from out of town."

"How's that?"

"The word is that she didn't leave town on her own, and Pug's the only one missing around here that I know of."

"Good point." I looked around the yard and beyond, but didn't see or hear anyone about. "Where are all you kids? It's too nice a day to be inside."

"They're at church with their mother. They go every Sunday. I go about twice a year."

"That's about my average, too."

"It's not that I don't believe and all. Well, you know how it is. Some of us just aren't church goers."

I told him that I knew how it was, thanked him, and left.

Chapter 12

I ate lunch at the Corner Bar and Grill, loitered there a while, and then left for the south end of town. More haze than cloud, the cirrus in the southwest did nothing to dim the sun, which so far was out of their reach. But they would thicken over time, and grow. That was their bent, their modus operandi. Move in gently at first so as not to alarm the natives, and then slowly, surely, insidiously, without mercy or regret, swallow the sun until no ray escaped, no light shone. I had been a cloud watcher all of my life. I didn't need a solar eclipse to tell me what doomsday looked like.

Tim Robinson lived on Railroad Street on the west side in the last house before you got to the railroad. Dewey Clinton, another odd duck, used to live there, but Dewey was long dead now, felled by the same one who killed Doc Airhart. The house was a two story white frame with a red brick chimney and an L-shaped porch, the length of which faced the south and provided a good place to sit, spring through fall. Not that Tim ever used it, but Dewey had in the past, whittling away the hours, as the wood chips flew. Dewey never made anything. He just liked to whittle. Tim never made anything, including friends. He just liked to stay at home and keep stats. As I said, two odd ducks.

Tim was home. I knew he would be. They were filling out the final brackets for the Sweet 16 today.

"What do you want, Garth?" Tim said when he came to the door. "As you can tell, I'm busy."

"Who's winning?"

"North Carolina. In a cakewalk."

"Then you won't be missing much."

"It's my time, Garth, not yours. I'm the one who decides what's worth missing."

"I'll be brief, then. How's that?"

He looked at his Rolex. "You've got exactly five minutes." Along with his watch, he wore red sweat pants and a white T-shit, and white athletic socks, no shoes. Sometimes he wore black slacks and black T-shirt, and a thick gold necklace when out on the town. But I could count those times on one hand.

"Emily Nelson," I said. "How well did you know her?"

He started to close the door in my face. I caught it and held on.

"Don't," I said. "Or you'll never get rid of me."

"Then I'll call the law."

"I am the law, like it or not. I can show you my badge if you want."

He took his hand off the door. "So the gloves are off now," he said. "I'm seeing the real Garth Ryland. And all the feel good, bullshit about our team was just that. Bullshit, to make us feel good, so we'd let our guard down. But I'll have to admit, you had all of us going for a while. Now that the word is out, see how far you get."

"You'll be eager to spread the word, won't you, Tim? Just like you did about Pug and Emily."

He tried to close the door again. This time I let him. There was nothing more to learn here.

The Pizza Place wasn't yet open for business, but I knocked on the door anyway. Doyle Nelson came to the door, saw who it was, let me in, and locked the door behind me.

"I'll be with you in a minute, Garth. I've got a pizza in the oven."

"Slunch," Heather Nelson said from her seat at the two-chair table beneath the serving window. "Our lunch and supper."

Heather Nelson had long, straight, sandy hair that she always wore down, tawny skin that never seemed to fade, even in the depth of a Wisconsin winter, light-gray eyes that always seemed either slightly sad or slightly amused, and a willowy body that she kept in shape by running 5 K's and mini-marathons. She always wore jeans and over-sized shirts in winter, shorts and halters in summer, some combination thereof spring and fall. She was a beautiful woman. I could look at her for hours without ruining my eyes. But we had never connected on any level except friendship. Some people are like that. Friends forever, lovers never. I guessed it had something to do with our stars.

"How are you, Heather?" I said.

"Not bad. How about yourself?" She kicked the chair across from her away from the table. "Have a seat."

"What about Doyle?"

"There are other chairs in here. He'll find one."

I sat down across from her, then took a moment to look around and reacquaint myself with the place, since

John R. Riggs

pizza wasn't often on our menu at home. There was sports memorabilia on the walls, that of the Packers, Badgers, and the Oakalla Braves. There were a few tables and chairs scattered around on the concrete floor, but no booths, and nowhere really to sit when the place filled up after a home basketball or football game. It wasn't small by design, but circumstance. The building was originally a way station when Madison Road was the main thoroughfare between here and there, and then for a long time, an auxiliary store for the cheese plant where they sold their wares locally. It'd had several owners since the cheese plant sold it, but no one had made a go of it until now. The Pizza Place was doing well, and would continue to do well until Doyle overreached himself, as was his MO, or simply got tired of it, which also had happened in the past. The one thing that Doyle had going for him this time was his inclusion of Heather in the business. Although not a ramrod, she was the wind in his sails, and the glue that held it all together.

Doyle came out of the kitchen, carrying a small Hawaiian pizza that he set on the table in front of us while he went to get a chair. The pizza looked and smelled good, and made the hamburger and fries that I'd had for lunch seem a distant memory.

"Help yourself," Doyle said. "There's plenty."

There wasn't plenty, but I took a small piece anyway. It tasted as good as it looked.

"So what brings you here on a Sunday afternoon, Garth?" Doyle said. "If you're looking for an apology, you have one. I don't know what got into me the other day. But something sure set me off. And as long as your here, I need some advice. What do you think about knocking out that

122

south wall and adding on? It would mean buying the lot next door, but I hear the cheese plant might be willing to sell if the price was right."

"I think it would be a waste of money," I said. "And the sure road to ruin."

When Heather gently kicked me under the table and smiled, I guessed it was the right answer.

But Doyle was crestfallen. "That's what Heather says. Any bigger, and we'd never fill the place. And most of our business is carry out anyway."

"Then I'd listen to her."

"Oh, I plan to. I plan to."

Which was a lie. In the end, Doyle Nelson always did what *he* wanted, no matter how much discourse to the contrary.

"Not to ruin your meal," I said, "but I have word from a good source that Emily might have been stalked by Tim Robinson. Is that true?"

"What does that have to do with anything?" Doyle said.

"Yes, it's true," Heather said. "He even used to drive by our place two or three times a day until I finally had to tell him to stop."

"It's a free country. You don't know he was stalking her," Doyle said.

"Yes, I do know he was stalking her because she told me. And I do know what such men are capable of because I have the scars to prove it."

"You've never showed them to me."

"That's because they're all on the inside, Doyle. I've not always lived in Oakalla, you know."

He held his hands up in surrender. "Whatever you say."

"Why the questions about Emily, Garth?" Heather said. "The last I heard, basketball was all the rage around here, and you were its head cheerleader."

"Her name came up in regard to Pug. It led me to Jared Cox, and he led me here. He swore he heard her say that she hated Tim Robinson. For my own peace of mind, I wanted to know if it was true or not."

"Jared Cox," Doyle said with a snarl. "I hoped I'd heard the last of him when Emily gave him the bum's rush, but like a bad penny, he keeps turning up."

"What do you have against, Jared?" I said. "Besides the fact that he's a gear head?"

"What don't I have against Jared? That's the question. I mean, be honest, Garth. What's he ever going to have in life beyond what he's got now? By the time he gets to be our age, all he'll have is memories. Of the good old days. When he was young and strong and invincible, and all full of piss and vinegar. Ask me how I know. I've been there, Garth. Except I didn't have three kids and a wife to support, like he does."

"Besides that, he was Emily's first, if you know what I mean," Heather said. "Doyle never forgave him for that."

"I should have had the son-of-a-bitch locked up. That's what I should have done. Would have, too, if Heather hadn't stopped me."

"It wouldn't have changed anything," Heather said. "Except maybe ruin his life."

"Well, he sure ruined ours. Or somebody did. If it weren't for Billy, I would have thrown in the towel long ago. I tell you, Garth, if anything ever happens to that boy, I don't know what I'll do. And I'll tell you one more thing. Anybody ever touches a hair on his head, they'll have me to

answer to. His or Howdy's either one. I love those boys..."
His voice trailed off... "I love those boys, that's all."

"Speaking of whom, where are they now?"

"Probably watching basketball with Marcus at Brooke's
place. But they'll be home by nightfall. And likely spend the
week together there at our place."

He looked at Heather just to make sure. She nodded yes.

"Do they do that often, spend a week together, I mean?"
I said.

"All the time in summer. But next week is spring break,
in case you didn't know," Doyle said.

I vaguely remembered Abby telling me as much last
Sunday, that "Praise the Lord!" She wouldn't have to teach
for a week. But that seemed eons ago.

"Thanks for reminding me," I said. Not that it changed
anything. Abby would be grading papers and working at
the hospital, and I had a newspaper to put out. Like a lot
of things on my wish list, spring break was just another pie
in the sky.

There was only one piece of pizza left. None of us would
be the one to eat it, so it went begging, even as Doyle picked
up the box and threw it away.

I rose. I had yet to broach my main reason for coming
and was running out of time and opportunity. So I took my
last best chance. "Speaking of hairs on his head, there is one
sure way of knowing whether Billy is Pug's son or not. Bring
me something of Billy's. I'll try to get something of Pug's,
and we'll match DNA."

"That's the craziest thing I ever heard of, Garth," Doyle
said. "I made my peace with that a long time ago, which
is why Howdy Hanson has always been welcome in our

house. I don't care who his father is. All I care about is Billy. Discussion closed." He went into the kitchen.

I looked at Heather for help, but got none. "I'm sorry, Garth, but it's his decision."

"Thanks anyway," I said, and left.

"How was the pizza?"

"How did you know about that?" I said.

"I can smell it on you."

"Not bad, if I say so myself."

Ruth and I sat in the living room at home, eating popcorn and drinking a beer. In the past we had shared a bowl, but I could never get the salt quite right and both of us suffered as a result. If I left it as I liked it, she invariably went into the kitchen for the salt shaker. If I salted it to her liking, I could barely eat it and spent half the night in the bathroom, filling up on water. A bowl apiece was the ideal solution. Too bad I hadn't thought of it years earlier.

"What do you know about Tim Robinson?" I said.

"Besides the fact that I don't like the man, what else do you want to know?"

"His taste in women, young women in particular."

"I didn't know he had any. Men either, in case you were wondering."

"Jared Cox swears that Tim was stalking Emily Nelson. Heather Nelson all but confirmed it."

"All that proves is that he has a pulse, which is more than I gave him credit for."

"He also says that Brooke Hanson was his girlfriend, until Pug stole her from him in fifth grade."

"And an imagination. I'm going to have to rethink that man. But I still won't like him."

"Why? He seems harmless enough to me. At least he did. A bit odd is all. But who around here isn't?"

"Because he got out of bed on the wrong side one day as a child and decided he liked it there. Some people bring you joy. Some people suck it right out of you. After I learned that lesson early on, the hard way, I've spent the rest of my life avoiding those who do. Some people delight in other people's misery. Tim Robinson seems one of them."

"What about Jared Cox? What do you know about him?"

"That he's lucky that he didn't marry the Nelson girl, and lucky he did marry the Stevens girl. That's about all I know, or care to know."

"It doesn't bother you that he was a twenty-year-old dating a sixteen-year-old?"

"Garth, my Karl was a twenty-year-old dating a sixteen-year-old. He married her at eighteen, and we had nearly forty good years together. I'm not going to pass judgment."

"Times have changed since then."

"True, but people haven't. We still think with our hearts. Sometimes to our regret. You, if anyone, should know that."

Someone knocked on our front storm door. "Are you expecting visitors?" I said to Ruth.

"No. Are you?'

I went to answer the door and was surprised to see Heather Nelson standing there. "Here," she said, handing me something sealed in a plastic zip-lock bag.

"What is it?"

"Doyle's hairbrush. He doesn't have much use for it anymore, so I use it on Billy. He has a cowlick that just won't lie."

"Why don't you come in?"

"I really shouldn't, Garth. If Doyle would ever find out I did this..." She let me fill in the blank.

"Why don't you come in anyway?" I thought I knew Doyle well enough not to worry about it.

She stepped inside, saw Ruth sitting there, and almost stepped back outside again. But Ruth had that effect on people, even when she was on her good behavior.

"Mrs. Krammes," Heather said with a nod to Ruth.

"Mrs. Nelson. Have a seat. Please."

Heather sat beside Ruth on the couch. Or appeared to sit beside Ruth on the couch. I could swear she was part way off the cushion at first, before she gradually settled in. After all this time Abby was still like that, always on pins and needles whenever she was around Ruth.

"I see you're eating again," Heather said to me. "Didn't we fill you up this afternoon?"

"He has a hollow leg," Ruth said. "He can eat more times a day than anyone I've ever known. And not gain an ounce. It doesn't seem fair, does it?"

"No," Heather said. "It doesn't." Then she went on to say to me, "I suppose you wonder why I'm doing this against Doyle's wishes?"

"It did cross my mind." I offered her my bowl of popcorn, but she shook her head no.

"It's as simple as this. Doyle might not want to know who Billy's father is, but I do. For Billy's sake, not mine. Try though I might, I can't see any of Pug in him, but if he and

128

Howdy are brothers, he really ought to know. I mean, they look so much alike, people who don't know any different assume they are brothers."

"What if Pug's not the father? Is that worth knowing, too?"

"Sure. Anything is worth knowing, as long as it doesn't hurt anybody."

Like keeping your silence when someone's long lost daughter lies in the trunk of a car a few blocks away? I doubted that would fit her criteria, or wash when the truth came out. Sometimes I hated myself and the badge I carried.

"And all that business about not caring who Billy's father is, is a crock," she said. "He cares plenty about it. He just doesn't think it is Pug. Neither do I."

"Who does he think Billy's father is?"

"He doesn't know. Neither would she ever talk about it to me. Emily could stonewall you when she wanted to, and go by her own rules. Whenever I would push her on something, she would always point out that I wasn't her mother, so it was none of my business."

"That must have hurt," I said.

"Like fury. But to keep the peace, you learn to live with it."

I could see Ruth bristle. Somehow Heather had struck a nerve.

"And as long as we're on the subject, Heather did hate Tim Robinson, and maybe even Pug for riding her so hard in basketball, but that wasn't who she was talking about when Doyle overheard us."

"Who then?"

129

"I don't know, Garth. I just know it wasn't them. This was after Billy was born, long after Tim quit coming around and Pug had left town." She looked at her watch. "I've got to go, Garth. I really do. The boys will be home any minute."

I got up to open the door. She hurried down the steps and hit the sidewalk running.

"The little rip," Ruth said a moment later.

"Who? Heather?"

"That daughter of hers. I've got two pet peeves— uncaring mothers and ungrateful children. I can't abide either."

"What about uncaring fathers?"

"Them too. But they're not usually the ones raising the children. More is the pity, in some cases."

I was hoping that would be the end of it. But it wasn't.

"Why didn't you ever take up with her?" Ruth said. "She seems more your type than some of the others."

"Heather you mean? Because she's married, and has been ever since I've known her."

"That never stopped you before."

"Why do you like her so? You hardly know her."

"I didn't say I liked her. I said she seemed your type. But I have to respect anyone who takes in not one, but two children, not her own, and loves them like her own."

"Emily and Billy, you mean."

"And the little Hanson boy. According to Liddy, he's there as much as he is home. It doesn't take a village to raise a child, Garth. But sometimes it takes more than one mother, or father. At least in my case it did."

"You didn't get along with your mother?"

130

"Let's just say that I'm glad that she had a mother, and that I had a father, and that he had a mother and father. I always had someplace to go where I was welcome."

She picked up a magazine and began to read. I finished the rest of my popcorn in silence, drank the rest of my beer, and went into the kitchen to think about my day.

Chapter 13

It was an unruly night. The wind blew hard out of the south, racing up the bare streets to rattle the trees and shake loose whatever dead limbs winter had spared. The moon came and went with the clouds that streamed across the sky in an endless sea of froth and billows that promised rain, but brought none. I was on my way to the shelter to see Abby. Tucked tightly against my side was the hairbrush that Heather Nelson had given me. Once beyond the lights of uptown, I felt like a running back who has broken the line of scrimmage and now awaits the footsteps behind him. My shadow was back there somewhere—following, waiting for his chance at me again. I knew that as surely as the route to the shelter and every house along the way. I feared not so much his guile or his persistence, but his intent. He meant to do me harm. And in his desperation, might also harm those I loved.

Once inside the front door of the shelter, I slammed the dead-bolt home and then went to the back door and then the basement door to make sure they too were locked. I didn't worry about the doors themselves. Each was solid oak, built to last at a time when lasting was important.

"What was that all about?" Abby said. She wore an extra-large gray sweatshirt that reached to her knees. Little else that I could see.

"Here," I said, handing her the bag with the hairbrush inside. "I need you to have someone run this as soon as possible."

"For what purpose?"

"To see if we get a match with Pug Hanson."

"What did you do to your ear?" she said, as she set the bag aside.

"I got too close to a helicopter."

"It needs stitches."

"I'll be fine."

"It needs stitches."

She went upstairs to her room and came back with a small surgical kit. She cleaned my wound, numbed it, and then stitched it in the time it would have taken me to put a bandage on it.

"So who shot you?" she said when she finished.

"Nobody. I caught it on a tree branch out at the farm."

"Garth, I worked emergency for two years in Detroit. I know what a gunshot wound looks like. So why all the secrets? We're not supposed to be keeping any from each other. Remember?"

"Because if this all goes south, which it very well could, I don't want you to take the fall."

"I've fallen before. I know how to get up." She held out the hairbrush. "Does it have anything to do with this?"

I owed her the truth. But with truth came trust, and that was hard for me, because, in the past, those I most loved proved the least trustworthy. Not with who I wasn't, but with who I was. Not with the me they had chosen to love, but with the me they could not.

"Okay. This morning, Danny Palmer and I found the remains of Emily Nelson in Pug Hanson's car, which was hidden under a drop cloth in Pug Hanson's shop."

"Then I need to see them."

"No. At least not tonight."

"Why not tonight? When will there ever be a better time?"

"Because whoever took a shot at me yesterday is right outside your door now. I might bet my life on that, but I won't bet yours. And, if you need reminding, you like to deal with live people better than dead ones. Well, so do I. Especially those I love. Emily Nelson isn't going anywhere tonight. And neither are you."

"But it's my job!"

"No. It isn't. It's Ben Bryan's job, and he's in Florida. Your job is live, so that you might help other people live, and give me a reason to come home at night."

"I'm that important to you, huh?"

"You'll never know."

We were in bed, but neither of us was asleep, when the front doorbell rang. And I was right about the sweatshirt. There was nothing under it.

"Don't answer it," I said, as Abby rolled away from me.

She got up and put her sweatshirt back on. "Garth, I have to. This is a *shelter*."

As if I needed reminded. I got out of bed and put my shorts and jeans on. "Then don't answer it until I tell you to."

We went downstairs. The first thing I noticed was how dark it was outside the front door.

"Didn't you leave the front porch light on?" I said.

"Always. You never know what time of night someone might need help."

I checked the light switch. It was turned on, but I flicked it a couple times just to see what might happen. Nothing happened. "Do you have any other outside lights that you can turn on?" I said.

"We have a front floodlight and a back floodlight. Which would you prefer?"

"The front. But wait until I tell you."

On my hands and knees, I went to the front window. When the doorbell suddenly rang again, loudly and insistently, I was ready for it.

"Now!" I said.

The instant the light came on, someone flashed into view, and was across the porch and down the steps before I could get a good look at him. Or her. It was hard to fix on such a fast moving target. I ran out the front door and down the porch steps to the sidewalk, but that was as far as I went. All would be well until he (or she) decided to turn around and start shooting at me. I'd bluffed him once. I doubted that I could again. Whether out of fear, or desperation, he might suddenly find a backbone. And, as luck would have it, his target.

"You were right. I was wrong," Abby said, once we were back in bed again.

"Small comfort that. Now he knows we're in this together."

"Somehow I find that comforting. Don't you?"

"Yes. As long as nobody is shooting at us. But I don't like taking chances with your life. Had I not come here, he wouldn't have come here. I brought him to your doorstep, and I'm sorry for that. But I needed to see you tonight. I take that back. I *wanted* to see you tonight. And every night hereafter."

"Same here. So quit worrying about it. I can take care of myself. Most of the time anyway. I am glad you were here tonight. But you keep saying he. Couldn't it be a she?"

"It could be. But I don't think so."

"Why not?"

"There's something erratic about him, that makes me think he's flying by the seat of his pants, or maybe someone else is pulling his strings. He seems to be making up a lot of this as he goes along. I don't think a woman would do that."

"Maybe you give us too much credit."

"Maybe. Maybe not."

She shucked her sweat shirt and threw it on the floor. I had already shucked my jeans and shorts. "Where were we?" she said as she rolled into me.

"We were about to make love."

"I thought we already did that."

"This is for all of the times we didn't. We have a lot of catching up to do."

She gave me a long warm wet kiss that shivered my timbers and gave rise to more than expectations. "We'd better get started, then."

At dawn I rode with Abby up to the Marathon in her blue-green Honda Civic. She loved to drive that car because it was "perky and reliable." I loved to drive that car because it wasn't Jessie.

Danny met us at the Marathon. He seemed relieved to now have Abby involved. That was because Danny was one of those people who took comfort in always doing the right thing. But I couldn't fault him for that. None of us is perfect.

"The remains match the description on her driver's license," Abby said as she closed the trunk lid. I'd say it's Emily Nelson. And that she's been dead a long time."

"Nine years long?" I said.

"It's possible."

"So what do you want to do with her?" Danny said, eager to be done with it.

"Leave her here for now. It's obviously a crime scene. I don't want it disturbed any more than it has been," Abby said.

"Until when?" Danny said.

Abby looked at me. It was my call.

"Give me today and tonight," I said. "If nothing breaks, we'll call in the state tomorrow. Nothing will make them happier than to relieve me of my duties."

"Do you think she'll be okay here until then?" Danny said. "I'd hate to lose her now."

"It's been nine years, Danny. One more day won't hurt. Besides, I'm about ready to go on offense, see what bushes I can shake."

"Okay, then," Danny said. "As long as she's out of here tomorrow. I'm tired of missing sleep because of her."

When I had called him earlier that morning on his cell phone, he was already at work. He said that he had spent most of the night here, watching Pug's shop, since Sharon and their kids were on their way to Florida. He'd also said that he'd had a late night visitor, a woman by the looks of her, but that she had fled once he turned the outside lights on.

A few minutes later, I kissed Abby goodbye, and she was off to Madison. A few minutes after that, I was on my way to work.

I spent a couple uninspired hours at my desk before calling it quits for the day. Already I had enough material for Friday's paper, and there wasn't much more coming in. There is nothing so old as yesterday's news. The air was out of the basketball, and there was nothing that I could do to change that, even if I had wanted to, which I didn't.

In a strange turn of events, the skies had cleared while I was at work, and the sun had come out. It wouldn't last, but it was nice to see my shadow again, walking boldly and confidently ahead of me into a rising wind that shook and shimmied the stop and the street signs along the way. It was tornado season in the Midwest, and had I been back home in Indiana, I would have been more than a little apprehensive about the day ahead; for back in my youth, it was on an early April day much like this one when monster tornadoes rolled across much of the state, ending lives as they leveled entire towns. But this was March, in Wisconsin. Although a tornado was not impossible at this time of year, the most we likely had to fear were house shaking winds and a few bolts of lightning.

As I entered Childers Drugs, I locked the door behind me and hung a sign that read "CLOSED, return in One Hour." Brooke Hanson soon appeared at the pharmacy counter in her white coat and teal turtleneck. No one else was in there. But then I had planned it that way.

"Good morning, Garth," Brooke said. "To what do I owe the pleasure of your company so soon after I saw you last?"

She was trying to keep it light, among friends, but I wasn't in the mood. "I have a few more questions to ask you about Pug."

Her face went from sunny to sullen. "And I told you last Friday that I was done with that. Enough is enough, for God's sake! Larry walked out of my life ten years ago. I want to move on!"

She was on the verge of tears. I couldn't blame her, but I had a job to do. Amend that. A mission that could not end in failure. I took out my wallet, opened it, and laid it on the counter.

"What's this?" she said.

"My badge. Read it if you like."

She read it. I didn't doubt that she would. "It says, *special* deputy."

"With all the powers of a regular deputy. Call the state police if you don't believe me."

"I think I will."

"Go ahead. I'll wait."

She considered it for a moment, then said, "No, I don't have time. I've got prescriptions to fill."

I tried not to let my relief show. Never on the best of terms, the state police and I had been on thin ice of late. Razor thin ice. Most of them from the local post hated my guts and wished me ill. The feeling was mutual.

"You said you had questions, Garth. Do I need my lawyer present?"

"If you like. He's two doors down."

"I was just kidding. Besides, I would never use Marcus as my lawyer. That would be too much like incest."

For some reason, the word struck always struck a nerve, perhaps because it carried so much negative weight, and once spoken, was so hard to retrieve.

"I'll try to make this brief, so you can get back to business," I said. "And as long as you answer my questions, it will be."

"What if I don't like your questions?"

"I don't expect you to like them. I just want you to answer them."

"Fair enough. Fire away. But if someone walks in here in the meantime, I'm done. And I mean that. Done. There's only so much I can take."

She thought the odds were in her favor. Little did she know.

"The first question is just because I'm curious. One of those he says, she says things, and I want your side of it. Why doesn't Howard ever go to see Barbara Hanson? Is that your doing, or his, or hers?"

"Because she never asks him to come. If you don't believe me, ask him. I tried, at least at first, to bridge the gap between them, but it soon became obvious that she wanted nothing to do with him. Why? Who says otherwise?"

"She does."

"Then she's a liar. Although I don't know why she would lie about something like that when it's so easily proven otherwise."

Neither did I know why Barbara Hanson would lie about it because, in this case, I believed Brooke.

"What about the rumors that Pug... Larry and Emily Nelson were seeing each other?"

"You mean shacking up, don't you, Garth? Say it like it is. You don't have to spare my feelings with euphemisms. He was screwing her in the back seat of his car. That's what I think."

"After practice, you mean?"

"When else would I mean? It's a small town. There aren't that many places to hide in. Besides the obvious. A house or a car. Take your pick."

Apparently she had never gotten out and about Oakalla as I had. I knew dozens of places in which to hide and the secrets they held. But she had a point. Pug's car would be the nearest and best place to go. If that's what they were doing. And so far I had no reason to doubt her. Unless one is a skilled actor, you can fake anger, but not hurt, which was still alive in her after all the years.

"Were you and Larry having problems?" I said.

"I didn't think so. At least no more than usual. You know, the normal, run of the mill stuff that always comes up after the newness wears off. Larry and I had been together forever, it seemed. So maybe the bloom wore off sooner than later, but it was nothing we couldn't fix. I think the fact that I couldn't get pregnant had a lot to do with it. Then he gets that little bitch pregnant, and there I am with nothing to show for seven years of marriage. How would that make you feel, Garth? Like crap. That's how it would make you feel. Like a sterile old woman."

"You didn't lose a baby early on?"

"No. Who told you that? Pug and I were very careful, at least before we got married."

Somehow I doubted that, but it wasn't worth pursuing. "A man hears what he wants to hear and disregards the rest." Same with a woman. We all were very good at fooling ourselves.

"One last question. It's a short one that requires a long answer. "What happened the night Pug left town? At least, what do you remember of it?"

"Why do you want to know?"

"So I can finish filling out my report."

"What report?"

"To the state police. I guess Friday's paper raised some eyebrows there. Now, they want to know if Larry should be treated as a missing person, so if in case he is, they can open a file."

"As of when?"

"They just called this morning, right before I came up here."

"So now the state police are involved. Maybe I should just talk to them."

"If that's the way you want it? Then I won't take up anymore of your time."

"That's not the way I want it. I just want to be done with it. Why can't I make you understand that?"

"Because the ball's not in my court anymore. Or yours, for that matter."

She looked longingly at the door for help, but no savior appeared. The sign on the door was holding serve for now. "Okay, in a nutshell, here's what happened. Basketball season was just over, so it had to be around this time of year. Larry usually closed at five, as did I, and if he wasn't coaching, we'd either eat at the Corner, or home, after work, depending on our mood, and our schedule. There was no Howard then, so we were pretty much free to do what we pleased, and with us both working, money was never a problem. I went home. I remember that much. And started supper. Spaghetti and meat sauce, I think it was, which was Larry's favorite, although I could never quite make it as good as she could."

"She being his mother?"

"Who else? Anyway, while I was fixing supper, I poured me a glass of wine. When I finished supper, I poured me another. Then, when Larry still didn't come home, another and another. Supper was ruined by then. The pasta anyway. So I dumped it in the waste basket, and then had myself a good cry."

"Had he ever been that late before?"

"Lots of times. You've never been married to a coach, have you? They keep all hours, which is why they are so hard to keep track of. And sometimes Larry would work late at the shop. Lots of times, actually. But that was usually after supper. And if he was going to be late, without fail, he'd call. So you can thank his mother for that, too, if you're taking sides in this."

"I'm not. Go ahead."

"There's not that much more to tell. At midnight, I called Barbara, knowing that she would be home from work by then. But she didn't answer. I called again at one, and she finally answered, on about the tenth ring, but she said no. Larry wasn't there. She sounded really strange, almost like she was in shock, but when I asked if she was okay, she snapped at me and hung up. The next morning, when he still hadn't come home, I called the state police to file a missing person report. So one of you is lying about that."

"But did they accept it?"

"No. They said to wait a while. In the case of someone like Larry, a healthy young white male, they almost always showed up somewhere sometime."

"Did you try to file again?"

"No. Once I got over the shock of it, I tried to move on, and have been mostly doing okay ever since. Until now."

"Then you have your answer. Neither the state police nor I are lying. They might have dropped the ball, but you didn't pick it up again."

"If you say so." She wasn't convinced. Or maybe she was just ready to be done with me.

"One more question. Did you happen to drive around town looking for Larry? Just in case," I said.

"After I talked to Barbara, I did. I drove straight there, but all of the lights were out and Larry's car wasn't out front, where he always parked it when we visited. So I drove to the school, thinking he might be there, then home by way of Emily's house. It wasn't there either, which came as no surprise. Doyle didn't like what was going on any better than I did."

"You and Doyle are friends, then?"

"That's two questions, Garth."

Then she came out from behind the counter, took down the sign, and unlocked the door, as a stream of customers poured in. I took that as my cue to leave.

I was home alone, sitting at the kitchen table, eating a peanut butter and honey sandwich and drinking a glass of milk. Ruth was pulling double duty at the shelter because Liddy Bennett's husband, Dub, was down with the flu and Abby was still in Madison, likely at the hospital by now. Although it was dark out, I had no trouble seeing the storm approach, as it lit up the southwest sky with one lightning bolt after another, some dropping from cloud to ground in long straight streaks that shook the floor and rattled the windows, others arching from cloud to cloud in nimble fingers of white that played about the far edges of the storm and gave its true measure. It was a monster. And headed right for us.

The phone rang. I groaned as I got up to answer it. Talk about timing, and irony. My last meal, and it's a peanut butter sandwich. Who said God didn't have a sense of humor?

"How's the weather there?" It was Abby.

"It's storming like hell." I held the receiver to the window. "See. So we'd better be brief."

"I bought you a cell phone. Remember? No way to get electrocuted unless you're in the tub."

"As if it'd be much help now."

"I can always call you back. But I don't know when that will be."

I ducked as a bolt hit nearby. Already I could hear static in the line. When it rose to a loud buzz, I would know it was time to hang up.

"Go ahead," I said. "But if you hear a loud bang on this end, and someone hitting the floor, don't bother to call back."

"Okay, long made short. There were three sets of male DNA on that hairbrush. None match that of Pug's. But here's the interesting thing. Two are a perfect match for each other."

"That stands to reason. It was Doyle's hairbrush. He's Billy's grandfather."

"Perhaps I should have explained better. The matching markers all come down on the male, or the paternal side. Like that of brothers. Or father and son. Or grandfather and grandson on the father's side. Or male first cousins from brothers with the same father on that side. You can trace generations that way. But to get a perfect match, it all has to come down on the paternal side."

It took me a while to to digest all that. Meanwhile the storm raged on.

"Garth, are you still there?"

"Still here. Thanks, Abby. What time will you be home tonight?"

"My shift ends at eleven. Unless I pull a double, I'll be home after that."

"Why don't you stay there tonight, so I don't have to worry about you?"

"I'm coming home, Garth. You're the one I'm worried about."

"I'll be fine. I always have been."

"Famous last words. Love you." She hung up.

"Yeah. Love you, too."

I waited for the storm to pass, then tried to call Heather Nelson at home. She wasn't there. I next tried the Pizza Place and got Doyle Nelson instead. "Is Heather there?" I said.

"Who wants to know?"

"Garth Ryland. I have a question for her."

"Garth, why didn't you say so? You're lucky you called when you did. I was about ready to close up shop. Business is dead, because of the storm and all. Can't say that I blame them, though. I wouldn't be out on a night like this, if I didn't have to be. There's another line of storms coming, in case you didn't know."

"I didn't know. Thanks, Doyle. Where is Heather by the way, if she's not there?"

"She took the boys to a show up at the Rapids. I think it was one of those superhero flicks that are so popular lately. I don't pay all that much attention anymore."

"On a Monday?"

"It's spring break, Garth. Just like summer, one night's as good as another. Besides, they might beat the crowds this way. What do you want with Heather?"

I couldn't very well tell him without giving both of us away. But my question couldn't wait. "Does Heather by chance ever brush Howdy's hair when he's over there?"

"All the time. You should hear the howl he sets up. He and Billy both. But she's one determined woman when it comes to their appearance."

"Thanks, Doyle. I appreciate it." I hung up.

147

But he called me right back. I was wondering how long it would take him to catch on.

"What's this hair business all about, Garth?"

"I'll tell you tomorrow. That's a promise. In the meantime, when Heather and the boys get home tonight, keep them there. And don't stop off at the Corner while you wait."

"And when did you start telling me what to do?"

"Don't be a hard ass, Doyle. Just do it."

I hung up for the second time. He didn't call back.

Chapter 14

The second storm wasn't as bad as the first, but then I didn't see how it could be. Now, a hard cold rain beat against the north windows and gave the house a chill it hadn't seen in days. I got in Jessie, drove to the east end of town, and parked outside my office. I would rather have walked, but not in the rain.

At midnight George Peterson and I were sitting at Barbara Hanson's kitchen table when she walked in the back door. "What a night!" She said to George. Then she saw me sitting there." What a night. And I have the feeling it's about to get worse."

"Did it storm in Madison, too?" I said.

"Did it storm? I thought the roof was going to blow off the plant. And you should see all the limbs down on the way here. And all the houses without power. I was grateful just to be home. Until now."

She plopped down between us at the table, all the fight drained out of her. She just wanted to get this over with, as did I. And there was no sense sending George to his room because for years he had been a willing accomplice. Or a reluctant one. It really didn't matter at this point.

"Tell me what you know," Barbara said as she lit a cigarette. "It will save us both time."

"Okay, here is what I know. I know Larry never left town the night he disappeared. I know he likely came here and killed himself, and you hid the evidence, as you have been hiding it ever since. I don't know why, but I'm sure you'll tell me. Do you want me to go on?"

"Please do."

"I know he's here right now, and if you'll just show me to his room, I'll prove it. Do you still want me to go on? I can come back with a search warrant if you like."

Cigarette in hand, Barbara studied me as she might a player who had just raised her in a high stakes game of stud. How much was fact and how much was bluff, and what, really, was my hole card? Much to my relief, she decided to fold.

"You got part of it right," she said. "But not the most important part."

"Which is?"

"Larry didn't kill himself. He had no reason to."

"His marriage was on the rocks, along with his reputation. He thought he might have Emily Nelson pregnant. He had never achieved his dream of playing big time college basketball, and now, after ten years, he was just marking time, waiting for the roof to fall in on him and his business. That seem like reason enough."

"Except for one thing. Larry couldn't have children. He had meningitis as a boy and that left him sterile."

"You know that for certain?"

"Larry did. He had himself tested after Brooke got pregnant for the second time."

"He showed you the results, then?"

"He didn't have to. Why are you making this harder, Garth? It's hard enough as it is."

"Then he knew Brooke was pregnant with Howdy?"

"Yes. And he wanted to make sure it was his before he took to raising him in what had become for Larry, a loveless marriage. They were just going through the motions, he said, and had been for a long time. He couldn't even remember the last time they slept together."

"And he never thought about leaving town?"

"Sure, he thought about it, especially with people on his case about that little tramp who got pregnant. But it wasn't his. It couldn't have been. Although I wouldn't have blamed him if it was. If a man doesn't find love at home, he's bound to go somewhere else looking for it. A woman, too, for that matter. Not that I have that problem." She squeezed George's knee. "Isn't that right, Georgy boy?"

For the first time since I had known him, George Peterson was at a loss for words. "If you say so, Barbara" was the best he could do.

"Did Larry ever say who he thought Billy's father was?" I said.

"No. He said he thought he had a good idea. But far be for him to spread rumors, seeing what they did to him."

"His life was still on the rocks. Why are you so sure Larry didn't kill himself? I mean, where was he going to go from here, a place where he had always had a place, and a place where he had always been?"

"For the same reason that I'm not a suicide, or you're not a suicide. He had too much fight in him to quit on life. He might have muddled through the next few years, but he would have come out all for the better on the other side. Had he been given the chance."

"Run me through that last night, then. The night you found him here."

"How can you be sure I did?"

"For the same reason you say he wasn't a suicide. Some things you just know."

Besides, my hour alone with George had confirmed that fact. But I wanted to take him off the hook if I could. I owed him that much. Probably more. Though I wasn't of the mind to thank him just yet. That could wait for the morrow—if we both lived that long.

Barbara got herself a cup of coffee, and then relighted her cigarette. I knew from my time with Abby that cigarettes and coffee went well together, along with cigarettes and conversation, and cigarettes and booze. Abby's worst moments now came on those rare occasions when we had the time to sit down and drink and talk. The rest of the time she was fine, as long as she didn't think about it.

Barbara said, "It was March, just about this time of year. You know, when your thoughts turn toward spring, even though you know it's still weeks away. I came home from work in a good mood for once, since my supervisor had called in sick, and was surprised to see Larry's car parked in front of the house, right about where he always parked it. Except there were no lights on inside the house, and I had turned one on when I left because I always do. Or always did before I got the timers, but that's still to come. 'Larry,' I called out. Are you here?' When I got no answer, I turned on every light I could find and started up the stairs. Only got part way, when I smelled it. A mixture of shit and gunpowder. I'm sorry, but there's no other way to describe it. Already I knew what I'd find, but I went on anyway. And there was Larry in his favorite chair, the one he used to sit in when he watched television, or played those video games he was so crazy about, with his brains splattered all over the ceiling and his grandfather's gun in his hand. In his lap really. His hand was just pretending to hold it. And there was a note beside him on the floor, saying how sorry he was for everything, and that he couldn't go on, knowing all the hurt he caused us. It was splattered with blood, along with about everything else in the room. It looked like his handwriting, but I knew better."

"Do you still have the note?" I said.

"No. I burned it that first night on the stove. Right after I decided what I was going to do."

"Which was?"

"Not let them get away with it. I'd burn in hell first. Right about then the phone rang, but I was in no shape to answer it. When it rang about an hour later, I bit the bullet and answered. It was Brooke, wondering if I'd seen Larry. She was worried about him, she said. I said no, but to keep me posted. My clothes were all bloody from where I'd held Larry, so I put them in the washer and began cleaning up the floor and the stairs where I'd tracked his blood. I was beside myself at that point, so afraid that someone would come before I was ready for them that I almost forgot about Larry's car out front. The keys were still in his pocket, so I moved my car out of the way, parked his in the garage, and then mine there in front of the garage. I was no sooner inside the house had turned out all the lights, when I saw a car drive slowly by out front. Then I had to clean up all over again. But this time in the dark. Well, by flashlight. It took me most of the night. I must have been half crazy. I couldn't do that again on a bet. But when that next day dawned, the house looked exactly like it did when I left for work, and that's the way it's been ever since."

"You just locked the door to Larry's room and left him there?"

"What else was I supposed to do, Garth? One peep out of me and the jig was up. Larry's death would have been ruled a suicide, and they would have gotten away with it."

"Who are they?"

"Whoever killed him. I always thought Brooke had a hand in it, but now I'm not so sure. She's one cool customer if she did. My biggest fear was that you would come calling. And now you have, although I can't figure out for the life of me how you put it all together."

I tapped my forehead. "Kidneys."

She gave me a harsh look.

"It's a joke," George said.

"I know it is. But I think I deserve a straight answer."

"You'll know before I leave here," I said. "Is that fair enough?"

"Fair enough. But I plan to hold you to it."

"So what happened then?" I said.

"Nothing. For the next few weeks. Which made me wonder what they were up to. I mean they had to know that I knew. But they couldn't do anything without giving themselves away. Then I came home from work one night to find every burner on my stove on. I mean, had I lit up the minute I was in the house, or come in smoking, like I usually do, the whole house would have been blown to kingdom come and me along with it. What saved me, I think, was that the redbuds were in bloom, and I put my cigarette out so that I could smell them. You know, one of those soft spring nights that remind you of your childhood. So I was on my guard after that. I never lit a cigarette until after I checked the stove first. That was just as well because in the fall of that year it happened again. This time they turned the thermostat down as well, hoping that when the furnace kicked on, it would set things off. That's when I decided that two could play this game."

George got up to pour us each another round of coffee. Already it had been a long night, and we weren't nearly done with it.

"I called a locksmith to change the locks and ordered a timer for my lights and security cameras the next day. A night or so after that, I got in Larry's car, planning to take it for a ride before I parked it. At least that was my intention, but it had other ideas. I really don't know how Larry drove that thing, Garth. I'd no more get going than it'd die on me, and when it did run a ways, it had no pep, like it was starved for gas. So I just parked it, long before I planned. In front of Brooke's house. Then I blew the horn and took off walking as fast as I could. Too late I remembered that I forgot to take the keys with me. The porch light was already on."

"Why Brooke's house?"

"She was still high on my list then. She still is. So it was either there or Doyle Nelson's house."

"Same question. Why Doyle?"

"On general principles, as much as anything. I never did like the man, after he sold me that goldbrick life insurance policy, and then the way he had it in for Larry, and wasn't shy about saying so. And I'd heard he was fooling around with Brooke when she was still in high school. A lot of reasons, Garth. But that was the end of it. They gave me no more trouble after that."

"Did you ever see the car again?"

"No. And I thought I'd seen the last of it. Until now."

Nothing more to learn here. And the night was slipping away. "It's time we went upstairs," I said.

"Do we have to, Garth? You already know what's there."

"Yes, Barbara. I think we do."

"I'll stay here, if you don't mind," George said. "I already know what's there, and I don't really want to see it again."

"It's your call," I said. "But Barbara might need your support."

"She has it. In everything but that."

He stayed where he was. I followed Barbara up the stairs.

Barbara sat on the floor beside Pug's empty chair with her arms around her knees and her knees pulled up to her chest, silently rocking to and fro. There were particles of flesh and bone within the dried blood spatters on the walls and ceiling, and blood stains on the floor and chair. And on Pug's trophies and ribbons and posters. Lying in the chair was the Luger that Pug's grandfather, Barbara's father, had taken off a dead German officer during World War II. But Pug never kept it loaded, she said, although it was loaded now. I helped Barbara to her feet, but that's as far as she would go.

"Give me a moment, Garth. This is taking some getting used to. It's almost like the day I found him. Only worse. Because now I know I'll never see him again."

"Take all the time you need."

I picked up the Luger, emptied the magazine, cleared the chamber, and put the shells in my pocket. "I'll be in the kitchen," I said, as I laid the Luger back down in the chair.

"You weren't supposed to do that," she said.

"I know. But this room's seen enough blood for one lifetime."

"It used to be a happy room, Garth." She followed me back down the stairs.

We were at the door. The wind was blowing hard against it, like a thing alive, wanting in. It was one of those nights not fit for man nor beast. Given my druthers, I would have driven straight home, and stayed there.

"I don't see how it happened, Garth," Barbara said. "I mean how Larry's bones ended up in your grandmother's root cellar."

I had my thoughts on the subject, but didn't share them. "When was the last time you were up there? In Larry's room, I mean."

"A few months ago. I didn't get up there nearly as much I used to. At first, it was a mother looking after her son. But over time, it was almost like I was invading his privacy, if you know what I'm saying. Kind of like it was when he went from a little boy to a man overnight. I had to learn new boundaries."

"Thanks, Barbara. I know how hard this is."

"Not unless you've lost a child, you don't."

"I did lose a child. A son. On his first birthday."

I opened the door and let myself out.

Chapter 15

The rain had changed to snow showers that came and went with the clouds. One minute the moon was out, and the next it was snowing so hard that I couldn't see fifty feet ahead of me. Jessie's headlights had never been very strong from the start, and over time they had dimmed to candlelight. That was why I rarely drove her after dark, and never for pleasure. Of course, the same could be said about daylight as well.

I drove to the north end of town and parked in front of Brooke Hanson's house. The front porch light was on, but that was the only light I could see. The house, like most of those in Oakalla, was two story with a large front porch and a small back porch that on most of the frame houses was no more than a stoop. Unlike most of those in Oakalla, this house was made of brick, brown brick for the most part, with a few blond bricks scattered here and there for contrast. It had once belonged to Roy Weaver, a banker. It now belonged to Brooke Hanson, a pharmacist. It was one of those houses that stayed in the family, even if the family wasn't blood.

I waited there in Jessie until her windows fogged and a chill set in. Finally, I had to move, so I went up onto the porch and knocked on the door. I was one of those people who rarely rang the doorbell or used a knocker, mainly because all of those back doors that I frequented as a boy didn't have door bells or knockers, so I never acquired the habit. Besides, I had an open door policy with most of their owners. If the big door was open, I went in. Where I was always welcome.

No one answered my knocks, not even after the third round. That wasn't good news, I didn't think. I expected Brooke and Marcus to be there. I tried the door. It was unlocked, so I went in.

There are those moments in every life when you know you are doing exactly the wrong thing, but you do it anyway. There is no logical reason for it, except, perhaps, to prove a point. You aren't a gambler or a zealot or a madman or a fool. Or over the rainbow or under the weather. You are just too fixed on your purpose to do otherwise. I had one of those moments when I went inside that brown brick house, unarmed and without backup. Every fiber of my being screamed at me to turn around and go back out before disaster struck. But I plowed ahead, like a mule on the edge of a cliff, too stubborn to stop.

The first room that I entered was an anteroom of sorts where shoes were left on the floor and coats were hung on wooden pegs. The next was a long hallway that led past the living room and the stairs on the right, and the spare bedroom on the left, then past the kitchen on the right, before it ended at the back door. There was a light on in the house after all. In the kitchen. I just couldn't see it from outside.

Brooke Hanson sat at the kitchen table in a pink nightshirt with her arms splayed out in front of her and her head resting on the table. There was a bitter twist to her mouth, almost like a snarl, and a wine glass standing just beyond her reach. She was dead, and had been for a while. Already she was cold, and rigor mortis had set in. And there on her slender, swan-like throat were the ugly yellow remnants of the bruises that Marcus had left when he had throttled her a week ago Saturday, and thus driven her to the shelter for help. Her mistake was ever going back to him. My mistake was not putting it all together sooner. It would have saved me a lot of grief.

Nothing to do now, but to sit down at the table and wait for Marcus to show up. It should have occurred to me that he might be already be there.

"She drank the Kool-Aid, Garth. I didn't kill her."

Marcus Milner came into the kitchen wearing jeans and a sweat shirt, dark circles under his eyes, and a two day growth of beard, and carrying a large caliber handgun on the order of my Police Special, safely locked away in my top desk drawer at work, along with my cell phone. Marcus didn't look too bad, everything considered, for a man who appeared to have been on an all day bender.

"Morning, Marcus. I guess that's what it is."

"Morning, Garth. I have to give Brooke credit. She said last Friday evening that you'd figure it all out and be coming for us. And now here you are."

I could smell whiskey on Marcus' breath, which made him all that more unpredictable, and my situation all that more perilous. At that moment, I didn't very much like my chances. But as long as he was talking, he wasn't shooting. And Marcus did like to talk, especially about himself.

"Is that why you decided to take a shot at me Saturday?" I said. "Brooke put you up to it?"

"Well, she might have pointed me that direction. But I figured the rest of it out myself." He pulled a chair away from the table and sat down, keeping his eyes and his gun pointed at me all the while. He wasn't about to drop the ball a second time. "See, I kind of knew your habits, and that you wouldn't likely be going to work on a Saturday, so it might do me well to hang around your place, and then go from there. And when I saw you get in your car and head out of town, I decided to follow you, just to see what might happen. When you pulled into that farmhouse, I thought well maybe, but I still wasn't sure. Not until you started down that lane toward the pond."

"Good of me to give you every opportunity."

"Except I hadn't shot my .222 in months, and it had been forever since I last sighted it. But I figured if I could hit a groundhog at a hundred yards, I could hit you at three hundred, or at least put you in the pond and drown you. What I didn't count on was how long it would take to get the range, or you charging up that hill after me. I thought you wouldn't do that empty-handed. Besides, I'd run out of shells by then. So I scooped up what brass I could find and took off." He studied me a moment, as if still not quite sure of me or what I might do. "What were you carrying, Garth?"

If I told him the truth, I might lose any advantage I had. "My .38 Police Special."

"And where might that be now?"

"Locked in Jessie's trunk. That's the name of my car," I said before he could take offense.

"Hell of a name for a car," he said.

"She's one hell of a car."

"Then why don't we go take a look at her. See what's in her trunk." It wasn't an invitation.

"We can go take a look at her, but not in her trunk. You need a separate key for that, and it's at home in my garage." Which was a lie. The trunk was unlocked and always had been.

"Why did you lock your gun in the trunk without a key if you knew you were coming here?" he said.

"It wasn't intentional. There are a lot of quirks about Jessie that you have yet to learn."

"Why don't we give it a try anyway. You first."

"What about Brooke?"

"What about her? She's not going anywhere."

"And if Howdy comes home in the meantime?"

"He won't. Before afternoon. He's spending the night with Billy, and neither one is an early riser. And I'll be back long before then to clean up the mess."

Back home, in Godfrey, Indiana, we had a man in town, a respected businessman, who would today be thought a pedophile because of his fondness for young men and boys. I always thought him harmless and treated him as such, even as he rubbed my back when I went in to collect my paper money. But my good friend, Dick Davis, who had seen him out at night, with hooded eyes and a growth of beard, said to watch my step. He was a different man after dark, and not at all the man he appeared to be in daylight. And although nothing untoward ever happened between us, I was always on my guard after that. Marcus Milner was such an animal, far different a man in shadow than in light.

"I told you it wouldn't work."

Marcus had tried Jessie's ignition key in the trunk to no avail. And in a stroke of luck, the snow that had settled on the trunk had frozen the latch, so it wouldn't work either.

"Get in," Marcus said, as he handed me the key. "You drive."

"Where are we going?"

"I don't know. I'll know when we get there."

Which meant that he was making it up as he went—as he had always done.

I had left Jessie parked facing north, which was the direction I went, until I had to turn east at the end of Home Street. It didn't take Marcus long to figure out that Jessie's heater didn't work very well, when it worked at all.

"Why don't you turn up the heat in here?" he said.

"It is up. As high as it will go. If you wanted heat, we should have taken your car."

"And leave your DNA all over it. No thanks."

We came to Fair Haven Road. I didn't ask which direction he wanted to go. I turned left. "Is that okay?" I said.

"Just drive. The direction won't really matter in the end."

Marcus was growing sullen. I decided to cheer him up. "When did you start following me?" I said.

"A week ago yesterday. At the shelter. I knew Brooke had gone there. And since she hadn't come home yet, I was starting to worry about what might happen—if she ever decided to cut her losses and me along with them. Then you showed up at the back door and then the next day at the Corner. I had to wonder what was going on, even though

Brooke said that she hadn't said anything. That her neck was in the noose as far as mine."

A wind gust raked the car, nearly pushing us off the road, followed by a blinding snow shower.

"Slow down," he said. "I'm in no hurry. You shouldn't be either."

I did as he said, mainly because I couldn't see to drive. "Then you left me for a while. Why?"

"I thought you were being straight about our team, just a simple, down home, feel good story about basketball and the boys who play it. I didn't want to overplay my hand if there was no need. You know what they say about letting sleeping dogs lie. Brooke had no such illusions. I should have listened to her."

"Whose idea was it to kill Pug?" I said.

"Brooke's. She said she would be ruined in this town once Pug spread the word about her carrying my baby. I said there was a simple cure for that, get a divorce and move to another town where nobody knew her, and I'd join her there later. But she wouldn't hear of it. She had a place in this town, and by God, she was going to keep it! You see what she named the boy, Garth. Howard, after her old man. That should tell you something. Daddy's girl, just like Pug was a mama's boy. Good riddance to both of them."

"You don't think of Howdy as your son?"

"I claim only one son, Garth, and his name is Billy."

Without asking, I turned left at Fair Haven Cemetery. Marcus might very well tell me to pull into the cemetery and park, but it was a chance I had to take. Lady Luck was still riding with me. He seemed not to notice, even when it got very still outside, as the church and cemetery, and the woods beyond, momentarily blocked the wind.

"How did it all go down, Pug's death, I mean?"

"Perfectly, we thought. She put something in his drink at home. Once he was out, I drove him in his car, carried him up the stairs to his bedroom, put the gun in his hand, put the barrel in his mouth, and pulled the trigger. Brooke had gone on ahead and had his room all waiting for us, including shells for the gun and a suicide note that she'd been working on for a week. Then we waited for his mother to come home, when we just knew the shit would hit the fan. And waited, and waited, and waited, until Brooke couldn't stand it anymore and tried to call. Twice, before she got through, and then, nothing after that. That old bitch outfoxed us, Garth. She's one tough bird. I can see where Pug got his grit from. So we had to take another angle, which was to blow her and the house up, but make it seem like an accident. An then they'd find Pug's body in the ruins, put two and two together, and we'd be home free. Except that didn't work either, and the next thing we know, Pug's car is parked in front of Brooke's house. Thank God the keys were still in it, so we moved Brooke's car out and parked it in the garage."

Speaking of home free, we'd passed the road to Mitchell's Woods without Marcus ever taking notice, and now were on the dead end road to Navoe Cemetery. Don't fail me now, Jessie, I pleaded, as you have so many times in the past.

"And Emily Nelson? Was that all Brooke's idea, too?"

"No. That was all me, Garth, and something that I never intended to happen. But she kept pushing me and pushing me to run away with her now that the baby was born. And when I said to be patient, that I wanted to work a few things out first, she said that she'd been patient long enough, that she'd waited until after the baby was born, just like I'd asked, and it was her turn now."

"She didn't care about Billy?"

"She cared about him. But she cared more about me. She was crazy in love with me, Garth. Not that I ever did anything to deserve it."

"Did Brooke know about you and Emily?"

"If not at the start, certainly in time. Pug knew. That was why Emily hated Pug so. Her read her the riot act once he found out about us. So that's why she never denied that it was his. It gave me cover and put him on the spot at the same time."

"Who started the rumor about Pug and Emily? Was it you?"

"Not me, Garth. I liked Pug too much for that. My guess is Tim Robinson. He'd always had it in for Pug. Ever since they were kids, Brooke said."

That was also my guess. But Marcus had a strange sense of honor. It was not right to bear false witness about a man you liked, but okay to kill him in cold blood. It was all a matter of convenience, I supposed.

"Why did you leave Emily's body in the trunk of Pug's car? More to the point, why did you leave the car in Pug's shop?"

"What's that, Garth? I'm thinking we might have taken a wrong turn somewhere. This isn't the road I had in mind."

He'd been paying more attention than I thought. His body language said as much, as he straightened and readjusted the grip on his gun, holding it in both hands now.

"I can turn around if you like. There's a cemetery just ahead."

"Don't bother. We can stop there." He relaxed ever so slightly. Just enough to give me hope. "As far putting Emily in the trunk of Pug's car, that was my plan all along. We'd drive out to one of the quarries around here. I'd kill her, put her in the trunk, and push the car over the edge and into the quarry. I'd kill two birds with one stone, and no one would be the wiser. Except that damn car kept dying on me. I thought there might be water in the gas, or that it had a bad plug wire, and the rain that had started to fall was only making it worse. So I pulled into the first lane I came to, the one where that big old house sits off the road..."

"Brainard mansion. We passed it a while back."

"And killed her there. Then drove back into town and hid the car in Pug's shop, where it's been ever since. It's funny, Garth," he said, "how hands that can take a life in the blink of an eye, can't even hold on to a basketball when it matters most."

Yards ahead was the short steep hill that led down to Broken Claw Bridge where it crossed Hog Run before the road dead-ended in Navoe Cemetery. I gave Jessie some gas as we crested the hill, then put her in neutral, which was Jessie's best gear, and at which she achieved her maximum speed, downhill with a tailwind.

On this night of serendipity, I caught another break. Another blinding snow squall hit just as we crested the hill and started down. The road was a white blur.

"You're going too fast for a gravel road. Slow down!" Marcus said, as he poked me in the ribs with the barrel of his gun.

167

"Bear with me. I'm having a little trouble here." I pumped the floor beside the accelerator as if it were the brake. "Shit!" I said. "We're going to have to bail."

In the instant that it took him to realize that Jessie's passenger side door no longer opened from the inside, I opened my door and jumped, yanking the steering wheel to the left as I did. It was then I heard a shot, right before I hit the ground rolling and pitched into the deep ditch there beside the road. Then I saw Jessie swerve as she reached the bridge and plunge toward the creek below. I heard, but never saw, her land.

Stunned, and bleeding from several cuts and scrapes, it took me a while to get my bearings, and decide that I was going to live after all. I knew that there was something wrong with my right arm. I didn't know how wrong until I tried to climb out of the ditch and couldn't raise my arm above my shoulder.

The climb down to the creek was a slow painful one. It was almost as far to the water from the bridge, as it was from the hill crest to the bridge. The one thing I had in my favor was that I was now out of the wind. It couldn't reach me there below the bridge, try though it might. And if I ever got that far, it would be at my back all the way to town.

Jessie didn't survive the fall. She had evidently flipped and landed on her roof, which was mashed flat with the top of her doors. Neither had Marcus Milner survived the fall. He had tried to exit my door, but been a tick slow, and Jessie had landed on top of him. All I could see of him was his hand sticking out of the muddy water, and a seam of blood, swirling out from beneath the car to join the roiling cascade in its rush downstream. "Know your enemy, Marcus" were my parting words to him.

What seemed hours later, I stood atop Broken Claw Bridge. On the hill behind me were the ruins of what had been Tillie Mertz's place. But Tillie was dead now, as was Ruben Coleman, who once lived in a shack beside the cemetery, as were so many of the people I had first known after I moved to Oakalla. Many of them one of a kind, who, when they were made, left behind a broken mold. I missed them, as I did all the characters that had passed through my life and given it meaning and color and substance. Sometimes I thought the present generation, with their faint hearts and onion skin, was an impostor, a pale imitation of the greatest generation that had raised me. But then again, I was a dinosaur.

Legend has it that on certain moonlit nights, while standing on the bridge, you can see the shadow of a skinny hand floating in the waters below, hence the name, Broken Claw. But I never had seen the hand. So when the moon came out from behind a cloud, I tried again. It was then that I felt another hand on my shoulder, like a father's hand there to steady and comfort me. But when I turned around, no one was there.

"Ruben, is that you?" I said.

No answer. I waved goodbye, and started the long walk home.

Chapter 16

Nearly two weeks had passed since Jessie took the deep six off of Broken Claw Bridge. Four funerals had been held in Oakalla since then, four burials in Fair Haven Cemetery. Brooke Childers Hanson was buried in her family plot alongside her grandparents. Larry (Pug) Hanson, Marcus Milner, and Emily Nelson had no family plots, so they were buried at random sites in the new part of the cemetery. Or so I was told. I didn't attend either the funerals or the burials. I was no good at solace and didn't need closure. I doubted that I would have been welcome anyway.

Ruth and I sat at the kitchen table, eating Sunday breakfast—bacon, scrambled eggs, and French toast slathered in real Wisconsin butter and real Wisconsin maple syrup. Daisy lay at Ruth's feet, her head on her paws and her eyes on Ruth, patiently awaiting the tidbits that she knew were bound to come her way. We were temporarily dog-sitting while Abby spent the weekend with her folks in Saint Paul. Hail! Hail! It was almost like old times.

"Why don't you want to live here?" Ruth said right out of the blue.

Here we go, I thought. There's no escaping it now. "Because you want to live here."

"No, I don't. I can just as easily live at the shelter. I spend most of my days there anyway. And come here in the evening to cook, and clean on Saturday, if you like. You're no good at it, and with the hours she keeps, Abby doesn't have time."

"You'd do that?" It was the ideal situation. Abby had broached it to me, but since I never thought it would fly, I hadn't mentioned it to Ruth.

"I just said I would. Of course, I'll need help moving."

The thought saddened her. It did me, too, so we dropped the subject for now. It was enough for me to know that I no longer had to worry about it. Abby was right. Sometimes I assumed too much.

"One thing bothers me, Garth, about this whole sad business. How did Pug's bones end up on your farm, and who followed you on that first day into town, if it wasn't Marcus Milner?"

"I'm hoping that will soon be revealed to me. I'll let you know for sure when I get home."

"So you're going out?" She seemed disappointed.

"For a while. If I can borrow your car?"

But her thoughts were somewhere else. "Where's Daisy going to stay? She's getting up there, you know. We both are."

"I'm thinking the shelter. She'd be good company for you. But that will have to be up to Abby." Who, I was sure, would agree.

"You really love her, don't you? Abby, I mean."

"That I do, Ruth." Although it wasn't something I liked to talk about.

"Why? What makes her different from all the rest?"

"Because it's easy with her. I don't have to work at it. Or wonder how much she loves me. Our difficulties have never been about us. Just logistics. Where she would eventually settle and take root. She chose Oakalla."

"She chose you."

"I could live somewhere else."

"No, you couldn't. And be happy. That's why out of all of them, I feel the worst for Brooke Hanson. She brought it all on herself, but to her way of thinking, she had no other way out."

"Why not Pug Hanson?" Who, as long as we were expressing sympathy, was my second choice. With Emily Nelson a close third. First place went to Howdy Hanson, who, without either parent, was now at the mercy of his grandparents, Howard and Dorothy Childers and Barbara Hanson. Never on good terms, they were currently not on speaking terms, and hadn't been for years. Wherever Howdy ended up, it wouldn't be where he belonged, which was with Doyle and Heather Nelson, and his brother, Billy.

"He had his moment in the sun, Garth, which she never did, standing in Pug's and her father's shadow for the most of her life. And he could have gone on from here and maybe done great things. But he didn't. He chose the short safe road, never realizing where it might lead."

"The same could be said for me, Ruth."

"Except you've not lived here all your life. You went out and saw the world, and then chose Oakalla as the place to make your stand. There's a difference, a big difference. The only question is, where do you go from here? Do you keep playing with fire until it burns your house down and everyone in it, or do you quit, and be satisfied to live a normal life from now on?"

"I quit."

"I'm not sure you can, Garth."

"I am."

A few minutes later I got in Ruth's yellow Volkswagen Bug and drove uptown. I'd had a pang of remorse the first time that I opened the garage door and Jessie wasn't there. After all, we had been through a lot together, and twice now, her eccentricities had saved my life. But that said, after all the years of aggravation and petty betrayals, I was ready to move on. I didn't yet know what my new-used car would be, only that it wouldn't be a Jessie, or a Volkswagen.

It's kind of hard to shift when your right arm is in a sling because of a broken clavicle. But I managed, soon pulling up behind George Peterson's small brown Toyota pickup with the camper shell in the bed. I imagined that he kept his black Ford 250 with its fifth wheel, the one he used to pull the big camper parked in Barbara Hanson's easement, in the former gas station next door to his taxidermy shop. But I didn't go look. I went straight into the shop where George was expecting me.

"You finally figured it out, huh?" he said.

"I finally figured it out. How's Barbara doing?"

"She's still sore at both of us. But I think she'll get over it. I hope so anyway, or it's going to be a long, lonely road for me."

"You could have handled it differently."

"So could you have. There's plenty of blame to go around, once you start assigning it. I call them like I see them, Garth. So do you. So does Barbara. Which is why I think she'll get over it."

The smell in George's shop hadn't improved any since my last visit. It still smelled like a meat locker, one with a chronic short in its electrical system. But it never seemed to bother George. I guessed that over time, like the lingering smell of death in Pug's bedroom, one could get used to about anything.

"When did you decide to move Pug's body?" I said.

"When I realized that nothing was going to change until I did. It's bad enough living with a ghost, Garth. But a body... Besides, I was never going to get her out of the house to do all the things we'd talked about, until it was gone."

"Why my root cellar?" Although I thought I knew.

"Because I knew you were the one person around who might do something about it, besides sweep it under the rug. I didn't know what, but at least you'd get the ball rolling, and I'd be off the hook."

"The brass padlock was a nice touch. So was the plastic cap over Pug's wound. They led me exactly where you wanted me to go."

George smiled at his own cleverness. "I thought they might."

"But you made one mistake when you reassembled him. Or was that intentional?"

"Give me some credit, Garth. I've been at this a while now."

"You wanted to make sure that I knew that Pug's body hadn't always been in that box, is that it?"

"That's it. I figured that you'd know that already, since his clothes were gone. But I wasn't taking any chances."

"Then you watched the farm, hoping that I'd show up?"

"Whenever I could. I just got lucky that one day, the day you found him. And when you and Danny went back out there, I knew I was home free. Or thought so anyway."

"Why did you switch vehicles between my visits?"

"Stupidity on my part. I got caught up in the game, thought I was a master spy or something. So when I saw your car parked at the Marathon, I drove over here and switched into my Toyota from my 250, which is about as easy to hide as an elephant in a soybean field."

"It probably can be done, George. Deer do it all the time."

"But not easily, I bet. Then I drove back out to your farm."

"Where did you hide while you were out there?"

"That abandoned farm just east of yours, the one with the row of pines lining the drive. It's easy to sit in their shadow and not be seen. And if anybody ever called me on it, I could always say I was looking to buy."

"You had it all figured out."

George pulled on the straps of his bib overalls and smiled. "Not really, but it did seem to work out. Not that I'd ever want to go up against you again."

"Why is that, George?"

"Because you go for the throat, and once you get hold, you never let go. A lot of people around here have learned that the hard way."

"Is that a compliment? Or a backhand?"

"Take it as you will, Garth. I'm going home."

On my way again, I drove north on Fair Haven Road with my window down, so that I might take it all in. It was one of those rare April days, when everything comes together—the birds, the trees, the sky, the flowers, the green of the grass, and the smell of the air and the warmth of the sun to create the illusion of heaven on earth—one of those days that make you want to look up and say, "Thank you."

I parked in the old section of Fair Haven Cemetery and began my walk toward the white pine that marked Rupert Roberts' grave. Rupert had died in February a few days short of his eightieth birthday, and he had been buried next to Elvira, his wife of fifty-five years, who had died in May, almost three years ago now. It's funny. You can go to the funeral and go to the burial. You can see the humped grave and the tombstone beside it. You can even be there at the end, hold someone's hand as he takes his last breath. But it doesn't hit home until you see that final date chiseled in granite. At least it didn't for me.

"I'm sorry it took me so long to get back here," I said. "But life got in the way."

Then I wiped away the tears, took out my wallet, my badge from my wallet, and buried it beneath his name. He had given me that badge. Together they would go to dust, which was as it should be.

About the Author

John R. Riggs is the son of Samuel H. Riggs (1913-2002) and Lucille Ruff Riggs (1918-2000) and the brother of C. A. Riggs, Prescott, Arizona. John was born February 27, 1945 in Beech Grove, Indiana, and in 1949 he and his family moved to Mulberry, Indiana, where they owned and operated Riggs Dairy Bar for a number of years.

John attended Mulberry Schools (1951-1961) and graduated from Clinton Prairie High School in 1963. He credits his teachers at Mulberry and Clinton Prairie for their direction and inspiration and for grounding him in the fundamentals of thought and action so necessary for meeting the challenges of life.

John then entered Indiana University, Bloomington, where he was a member of Lambda Chi Alpha fraternity and rode in the Little 500. While there he earned a BS in social studies and an MA in creative writing. He later attended the University of Michigan, studying conservation and environmental communications.

On September 2, 1967, John married Cynthia Perkins (1945-2002), and their children are Heidi Zimmerman, Mansfield, Ohio and Shawn Riggs, Colorado Springs, Colorado. On July 1, 1988, he married Carole Gossett

Anderson and their children are Flint Anderson, Coatesville, Indiana and Susan Shorter, Spencer, Indiana.

Since 1971, John has lived in Putnam County, Indiana, currently on a small farm southeast of Greencastle. While in Putnam County, he has worked as an English teacher, football coach, quality control foreman, carpenter, and wood splitter. From 1979-1998 he assisted James R. Gammon of DePauw University with Gammon's landmark research on the Wabash River. He recently retired from DePauw University Archives, but continues to mix chemicals for Co-Alliance, Bainbridge.

John is the author of 17 published books in the Garth Ryland mystery series, and the 2001 Bicentennial History bulletins for the Indiana United Methodist Church. He has also written River Rat, a coming of age novel; Of Boys and Butterflies, his ongoing memoirs; and numerous essays. Me, Darst, and Alley Oop, a travel odyssey and his first extended work of non-fiction, was published in 2016

Printed in the United States
By Bookmasters